Jaguar and Grizzly

Apex Investigations: Book Two

Julia Talbot

Julia Talbot

Jaguar and Grizzly

Cover illustration copyright Kanaxa

Used with permission

Published by Turtlehat Creatives: August 2019

 Created with Vellum

CONTENTS

JAGUAR AND GRIZZLY

A client with a cheating wife, a warehouse of cult members, and someone with a deadly vendetta—just a day's work for Apex Investigations. Or is it?

Bear shifter "Grizz" Locke is ex-military and ready for PI work, which if not exactly safe seems less likely to get him killed on a daily basis. The added bonus of teaming up with former lover, Brock, a jaguar shifter, is all the incentive Grizz needs.

Brock can be a grumpy kitty, but has found a home and family at Apex. And now as luck would have it, he has a chance to rekindle his romance with Grizz. They might even rebuild their mate bond, severed years ago—as long as they don't manage to get killed first.

When an enemy targets the Apex team, Brock and Locke will fight with all they have to protect their own. To enjoy life and love as fate intended, they will have to find out who wants them dead before someone at the agency pays the ultimate price.

APEX INVESTIGATIONS READING ORDER

PROLOGUE

Mick Hartness hated it when one of his own investigators was his first appointment of the day. Hated it.

If they needed to make an "appointment," then it always involved bitching and moaning and "oh, the shifter humanity" and shit.

Frankly this Friday morning should be pissing and whining free. He hadn't had enough coffee or doughnuts to deal with Brock, especially. Brock could chew some scenery when he was upset, roaring and tossing furniture, and in this office it was still all new.

The knock came precisely at nine, and Mick sighed. Ready for battle. "Come on," he barked.

Brock came slinking in, wearing a black hoodie, black sweats, and a vicious black eye. His attitude matched his clothes and face. Impressive.

"Who smacked you?" Mick asked, trying to keep it casual.

"Client. Didn't appreciate my assessment of the situation he asked me to assess."

"Oops." Shit. He'd have to ask Carrie to check in with the client, see if they were still on the case or no. They had the retainer, regardless. He scribbled a note on his blotter. "Is that what we're meeting about?"

"*Não*. I'm here about Locke. He's looking for work, but he's a bear. You know how they are. Pouty."

Like Mr. Kitty wasn't pouty. And bears tended to be rather happy-go-lucky, in Mick's experience.

"Uh. Okay. So what's that got to do with me?"

"Uh, you're the boss. I'm not about to step on toes by hiring his hairy ass."

"I said...." Mick frowned. "Well, I guess I said we would hire him at the end of the Patel thing, but he never came in to really apply."

"He stayed at the house for a while and then pulled cleanup for us."

"But I mean he never came here. To interview or get an assignment," Mick said, growling some. "Get his ass in here."

"I know. He's... intense. This job, though? Perfect for him." Brock waved a file.

"That the one who hit you?"

"Yep. If he hits me again, I'll kill him. There's little chance he'll hit a grizzly."

"Mmm." Mick wondered what the hell Brock was up to. Usually he jumped at the chance to kill someone. "So you decided to spare his life because...?"

"I assumed with all these new bills, you wanted to get paid."

"I do." Mick chuckled, then winced at the sound of hammering just on the other side of his office wall. "I swear, those beaver friends of Rey's are great workers, but I'll be glad when they get all the reno done."

"Beaver friends...."

"Stop it. You're still sucking up over Rey."

"I am not!" Brock's chin jutted out. "I don't suck up to foxes."

"Yeah? Who brought him rum raisin ice cream yesterday?" Rey was the newest member of their Apex Investigations team, a fox shifter who'd been a client. He and Brock had... gotten off on the wrong foot.

In a vaguely desperate, drippy, funky way that had involved dire croc shifters.

Brock's lip pooched out too. "I brought you and Dylan butter brickle and mint chip for Kit too."

"Sure. Sure. Nothing special for the fox. Except it was Häagen-Dazs to our store brand." God, this was fun.

"Like you dogs know the difference. You'll eat anything."

"Hey, no one dumpster dives as bad as Kit." Their resident black bear could put away the food. Crap food too. All of it.

"Don't remind me. He's still banned from my SUV. For life."

"Yeah." Mick wheezed, he was laughing so hard. He held out a hand. "Give me the file, then call in your buddy. I'll meet with him ASAP."

"Thanks, boss." Brock actually unbent enough to smile.

"Did you have Kit look at your eye?" Mick asked.

"No."

He growled softly. "Maybe you didn't hear me. Go have Kit look at your eye." He was the leader of this team, which meant he got to snarl and demand and give orders.

"Well, when you put it that way...," Brock said, supposedly meekly. He rose, tugging out his phone. "I'll call Locke."

"Tell him to bring all his info." They would need the relevant paperwork if he wanted Locke to start now.

"Will do." Brock swirled out of the room as if his kitty tail was there to swish.

Mick grabbed his cell and called Kit. His "even newer than the hated one that had been destroyed with their last building" desk phone was too damn scary. But by damn, Kit was going to look at Brock's black eye.

ONE

P addy "Griz" Locke smoothed his hands down the front of his shirt. This was a job interview, after all. He'd compromised on the tie and jacket by wearing a pair of gray slacks instead of jeans. He was big and burly. Formality didn't suit him, but he could clean up all right.

The little fox that they'd found after a kidnapping on the job he'd done for Apex was sitting in the new lobby, talking to a lovely young wolf, both of them animated and laughing.

Locke cleared his throat.

"Oh! You're Locke, right?" The blonde stood, smiling at him. "I'm Carrie, Mick's assistant."

"Hey, Locke." Rey waved. "Break a tie—what's better, *X-Files* or *Supernatural*?"

"Oh, *X-Files*. It was the OG, man. Like *Buffy* trumps all the newer vamp shows."

"Oh...." Carrie fluttered. "*Buffy*."

Rey nodded sagely. "*Buffy*-thon. I'll tell James and Kit."

"Cool! You're welcome here, Locke. Is it Locke, or is it P—"

"Locke." He shook his head. He'd emailed his deets, so she'd seen his name. Lord. Paddy. Paddington. Just no.

"Yes, sir. Come on back. The boss is waiting." Her heels clicked on the floor.

"Thanks." Locke tried to think unsweaty thoughts. He'd never had an interview in his life. He'd been recruited out of the military to do wet work, but he wasn't getting any younger, and black ops was a dead-man's game anyway. PI work seemed, if not safer all the time, less likely to get him dead on every assignment. So... he could learn to sit and answer weird questions about his strengths and weaknesses.

Besides, working with his oldest friend, Brock, had... possibilities. Even the location seemed new and shiny. What better place than the Mile High City for a grizzly bear? Well, okay, ideally Alaska or something, but Denver worked.

Carrie led him to an office all the way in the back, the door kind of imposing, solid wood with Celtic carvings. *Neat.* Mick had good taste. She knocked, then opened the door. "Boss, your appointment."

"Thanks. Come in and sit down," Mick barked. "Why the hell didn't you come in before now? I told you we would hire you."

"People say things in a stressful situation." He'd asked, sure, but he'd thought Mick was just being kind.

"Well, not me. I mean it. Now, I still had to look at all your shit, so bear with me." Mick bared his teeth more than smiled. "Pun intended. Paddy? Really, man?"

"Not my fault. Mother has a terrible sense of humor." Paddy Locke. Paddington Bear. He'd been teased for years. A lot. Until he got too big to tease.

"Yeah, the only reason I despair is Locke and Brock. Still, the guys will give you a nickname. It's inevitable." Mick waved a hand. "Anything that makes you crazy? I need to know what kinds of cases to assign you."

"I'm good at stakeouts, at surveillance. I'm damn patient. I'm not techy. At all." He could do basic stuff, but high-powered listening and cameras and shit, not so much.

"James is our tech guy, and honestly, I think Rey can back him up anytime. Dylan has been the only one willing to do the real gumshoe stuff you mention, so hallelujah. He's a little overwhelmed. New mate and all." Mick raised one shaggy gray brow. No way was the guy old enough to be that gray, so his wolf must be a gray wolf. That would explain his imposing physical size too.

Not that Locke was small. Grizzly bear, ahoy!

"Mate bonds can be intense." He knew all about that. It had taken years for him to understand that not everyone called to mate managed to do it.

"So they tell me." Mick rolled his eyes. "Anyway, what's your favorite fast food?"

"Arby's." He loved the chicken salad sandwich.

"Good to know." Mick made a note. "We do a lot of, uh, team building through food."

"We're predators. We're made to hunt and eat." And fuck.

"Exactly." Mick nodded, as if making a decision. He pulled a file out of a drawer in his desk. "Brock dropped this one like a hot potato, so now it's yours."

"What did Mr. Kitty do now?" Brock had a temper; Locke could only imagine.

"I don't know, but the client is hostile. Punched Brock in the face." Mick's scowl spoke volumes. "You only take so much shit. If the client can't play nice, cut him loose."

"Fair enough. Wolf, I assume?"

"Yeah. Cats and dogs." Mick rolled his eyes. "I thought since it wasn't a fox, we would be good."

"Don't. I'm still shocked he hasn't killed little red." Brock had bad history with a fucked-up fox.

"Rey is winning him over." Mick chuckled, shaking his

head in a fond way. Then he picked up his cell to text something. "Carrie will take you to your office."

"Thanks." He stood, held out one hand. "I appreciate the job."

"Do me proud." Mick stood as well, shaking his hand firmly.

Carrie knocked. "Hey, come on. Welcome to the team. Do you know everyone?"

"I do. We've all met. Bear, kitties, wolves, and fox."

"Yep! Rey is great, and I love bears, so we'll get along great. You have an office, but it gets painted tomorrow. It's just here. Do you mind sharing with Brock until then?"

"No problem." They had figured their shits out, right? Brock might not want him or anything, but they could be buddies.

"Good deal. If you have a color preference for your office, holler before five. Otherwise it will be cream."

"Green. Green, please. Something deep and good."

"You got it. Soothing and yet creative." She bounced. "See? I knew we'd get along."

He grinned at her. That woman was joyful. He approved. Life was too short to be all grumpy all the time. Like Brock.

Carrie knocked on Brock's door. "Yoo-hoo, kitty. Locke needs to share until after they paint tomorrow. You have the space."

"Sure. I'll be in the gym most of the day." Those green eyes were hidden under a hood, the lean body merely a shadow. "Welcome aboard."

He fought not to roll his eyes. Mr. Ghost Kitty. "Thanks. Thanks for the way in."

"Anytime. You know I—enjoy working with you."

Goddess, that low, rippling voice was like silk. Made him shiver. Hell, it threatened to make him hard. "I know." He nodded to Miss Carrie and went to sit, letting the door close behind them.

"So, did you get the Hetrick file Mick sent you?"

"I did. Why did he clock you?" He wanted to see Brock's face.

"Wolf with anger issues. He wants to Alpha someone. Idiot."

"He chose poorly." Locke studied the stiff set of Brock's shoulders. "Look, I can just go set up at home until tomorrow is over."

"Why? We've worked together before. We've worked together a lot. What's different now?"

"Because you're already avoiding me." He sighed, knowing he shouldn't want more from Brock but wanting it anyway.

"I'm avoiding the world." Brock pushed his hood back, exposing a violent bruise. "Broken eye socket."

"Shit, man. That's a hellacious strong wolf."

"Yeah, God help us if he forms a pack." Brock shrugged.

"Fuck working out. Come sit and fill me in. I'll order a pizza."

"Marco's."

"Is that close?" He wasn't as familiar with the area, but he knew the name.

"Yeah. New York style pie." Brock actually smiled.

Oh, that was hot as hell. "Sausage?"

"Please."

"You got it." Locke would do just about anything to see that smile. He was such a sucker.

Brock came to him, close enough for him to smell. *Oh, kitty.* God, he loved that musky male odor. So much.

Brock sat damn near in his lap, pressed against his arm.

Give me strength, he thought. He opened the file, ready to walk through it with Brock.

The wolf was big, the look on the asshole's face grumpy as fuck.

"What's his deal?" Locke stared, trying to get any kind of feel from the pictures.

"He's convinced his wife is cheating on him with his business associates."

"Business associates?"

"Uh-huh."

"How many?"

Brock chuckled. "How many associates does he have, or how many does he think she's sleeping with?"

"Oh God."

"Yep."

It was no wonder Wolfy and Brock had come to blows.

"How many is she actually sleeping with?" Locke asked.

"Three. One human couple and a bobcat."

"A couple?" Locke blinked. "And you told him that?"

Brock's green eyes twinkled. "Nope. I told him about the bobcat."

"Ah. Male or female?" He wanted to know what the guy objected to most.

"Male. Hot little stocky shit, but I never have gotten a good pic of his face."

"Mmm. Yum." Brock was the yummy one, and Locke dared to lean closer, nose moving.

"Yeah, he'll fuck anything that moves." Brock watched him, interest flaring in those green eyes. "Me? I'm picky."

"Are you?" Griz hoped that was true. He liked the idea of being Brock's type again. A lot. It had been... years.

"I am." Brock blinked once, slowly, and Locke swore he could see those whiskers twitching.

"Well, I am too. I really like green eyes...." God, what was going on? He and Brock had been so careful to avoid each other, by Brock's command. What the actual fuck was going on?

"Do you? I've been burned by them. I like dark these days."

"Uh-huh." Locke's eyes were dark. That was good.

"I need to...." Brock leaned in toward him, but the office door blew open, and Brock seemed to fly back to his chair behind the desk.

"Dude! I heard that Locke was coming. Hey, man." Dylan, the boss's second, stood there, one hand out.

"Hey, Dylan. Nice to see you." Go him, standing and shaking hands without roaring and ripping Dylan to shreds. His bear was.... Right. There. Mad about losing out on maybe a kiss.

"So glad you're here. We're talking about all going to get subs for lunch. You two interested?"

"Sure." Brock was back to guarded in an instant, and Locke was pretty sure he liked Dylan.

"I promised Brock pizza. We have to review this file." He'd been so close....

"We could have pizza tonight, put our heads together," Brock murmured.

"Oh." Locke blinked, and then a grin stretched his cheeks. "That sounds good. Great."

"Yeah." Brock's smile was barely there, but it was there, glinting.

"Cool!" Dylan looked back and forth between them. "So, give your sub order to Carrie, huh? I'll see you in the break room."

"Right, bear, you want tuna?" Brock asked.

How did anyone make tuna sound sexy? "Uh. Yeah. A tuna and one of those teriyaki chicken ones." Locke could eat a mountain of food.

"Mmm... I like turkey and double cheese."

Cheesy kitty. Brock loved that salty hit of provolone. A lot.

He smiled over at Brock. He could wait to share a private pizza. Tonight.

Brock grinned back, looking damn near just like the day they'd first met, and his heart clenched. God, he—that face made Griz happy.

He thought he made Brock happy too. In fact, he thought that was the problem. That scared the fire out of his wounded jaguar.

Brock called in their order to Carrie, then turned to him. "Come on. There will already be food of some kind. I'll show you where the break room is. It's more like an airline VIP lounge, I swear."

"Do you have a place here now?"

"I do. I like to keep my house sacrosanct."

"Yeah." He wondered what that meant. Oh, he knew the word. He just wondered what it meant to Brock. "Still, it was good you let the guys stay there after the crocodile thing."

"They're my family."

That was a hell of an admission from Brock.

The temptation to ask what he was to Brock felt huge, but Locke pushed it back. They headed out from the main office, then downstairs.

There was a large, open break room, something meant to keep the Apex PIs at the office. Hell, the place had a pool table. Locke had a feeling he would be down there a lot. He liked to shoot pool while he thought about things.

"Spiffy," he muttered.

"Isn't it?" Brock chuckled for him. "I knew you'd like the pool table."

"I do. Wanna get in a game while we wait for food? Or does the new guy go pick up?"

"I bet Dylan and Rey go. They'll make out while they wait."

He hooted, which made the other bear ask, "What did I miss?" when he walked in.

"Hey." Locke lifted a hand.

"Hey! Fellow bear man! Welcome." Kit was on him in a heartbeat, engulfing him in a huge hug.

"Hey there, little bear." He hugged Kit back, greeting one of his own.

Kit chortled. "Only you would call me little."

"Maybe a polar bear," Locke suggested.

"True. Have you ever met one?"

"I have. There was one up in Montana who did polar rescue...."

Kit stared at him, enrapt. "Oh? Was he huge? Was he an albino? Was he amazing?"

"He had white hair and gray eyes. Which was crazy, because he had brown eyes as a bear. Like, almost black."

"Wow."

Brock watched Kit with a quiet, almost gentle fondness. Definitely family, though Locke's short acquaintance with Kit told him people reacted to the guy that way. He was a sweetheart.

A sweetheart who could decapitate someone with a single blow.

He grinned. Bears. Locke did love his kind.

"We were about to shoot a game," Brock said. "Wanna play, Kit?"

"I'll watch. *Jurassic World* is on, and I love the part with the raptors."

"It's oddly hot," Locke agreed. How did anyone work here?

"Bears, bears, bears. So, are you going to go snap pictures of the lascivious Mrs. Hetrick?"

"I am." He would give the wolf proof, not just information. Maybe that would save him from a black eye like Brock had.

"She likes to get out early in the morning and in the afternoon." Brock looked amused.

"When he's not around, huh?" Locke chalked up a cue while Brock racked.

"His problem is that he's bucking to create a pack and be an alpha, and he's terrified that she's going to ruin his chances."

"She is." That came from James, who wandered in, munching from a bag of Cheetos. "She's cray-cray."

"Is that an official diagnosis?" Brock teased.

"It is from what I can see. I mean, I looked at the files and all. She's had something like fifteen affairs in two years."

"That's one unhappy woman. I feel sorry for her," Kit said.

"Which is why you're not on the job." Mick's growl filled the air around them. The boss could really bark.

Kit whirled and stuck out his tongue at Mick. "Right. I'm a softie."

"You are, but you're an effective softie."

"Oh, good." Kit winked broadly, causing them all to chuckle.

"Break, would you, Locke?"

"Sure." He lined up, his eye training right along the line he wanted the cue ball to follow. He shot, the balls breaking with a satisfying crack. Three balls went in.

"Solids," Locke murmured, taking two more balls before missing.

"Another hustler...," Mick muttered.

"You put in the table." Brock was purring with laughter.

"I did. I put in the PlayStation too."

"Too bad you suck at games," Kit said cheerfully.

"That's for you and Dylan. Even Rey."

"Where are Dylan and Rey?" Locke asked. "Dylan came to get us."

Heels clicked on the floor, Carrie joining them. "They went to pick up the subs."

Brock's lips curved. "Told you."

"Ooh. *Jurassic World*!" Carrie fluttered. "I love that one."

Locke laughed, bemused as hell. No working environment had ever been like this.

This was like a frat house with guns and coffee.

Mick winked at him, making him laugh again. Then he saw something out of the corner of his eye. "No cheating, Brock."

"I would never." Brock's laughter slid down his spine.

"He so would!" Kit called.

"I'll bite you, little bear!"

Oh, Locke didn't think so. No biting anyone but him. Before he even thought, he drifted between Kit and Brock.

He swore he heard Brock purr louder.

His body tightened, so he focused on the game, on his shot.

He took it, sank two of his balls. Yeah. He still had it. God, he never played anymore.

Brock missed his next shot, and the kitty goosed Locke on his next one.

Full contact billiards. He loved it. Maybe they could play again later tonight. He would bet Brock would love that. Unless he had better things planned. More exciting things. A bear could dream.

Of course, they already had pizza planned, didn't they? Pizza. Just the two of them. He wanted to dance. Too much to hope that Brock suddenly had a real change of heart. But maybe he could get to be Brock's friend again.

He thought they had started on that path, not too long ago.

Brock looked at him suddenly, smiling a smile that seemed to be just for him, and he had to move to stand in front of the table to hide his hardening cock.

"Your shot, Griz."

"Right." He circled the table once. Two balls left. The five and the eight. He sank the five, but bounced the eight off the rail in the wrong spot.

"So close." Brock managed to sink all his balls and the eight. "I win."

"Oh, butthead."

"Food's here!" Kit crowed when Rey and Dylan came into the break room.

"Finally!" Carrie stood, moving in like a hunting wolf. "Starving."

"There was a line at the sub place," Dylan muttered.

"What? A make-out line?" Kit teased.

"No, a real one. It's lunchtime."

Rey was bright red, though. Those copper eyes were dancing with laughter. He thought Rey was wicked under the sweet, quiet exterior.

"Are you suggesting you two didn't get it on in the car, foxy?" Brock teased.

"I am not suggesting that, at all." Rey sniffed, then bounced over to hug Brock, which was seriously hilarious. Brock always froze, then hugged back. "Come eat, kitty. I got you two with triple provolone."

"You are good to me." Brock purred softly.

Luckily, Locke didn't have to be jealous of Rey. The little fox was mated, well and truly.

No, the other bear was competition, maybe, although Locke didn't think so. Kit really seemed to be oogly for Mick.

Or maybe that was just childish admiration and Locke couldn't tell the difference anymore.

It didn't matter. What mattered was his dark jaguar and bringing them together. Somehow.

Even if he had to do it with provolone.

Two

"How's the eye, friend?" James came into Brock's office, carrying an ice pack. "Congrats on bringing the grizzly on board. He's got a great résumé."

"He's a good man." Dangerous. Possibly heartbreaking for him, but good for business. "Thanks."

He leaned back and put the ice pack on his eye. *Fucking asshole wolf.* If it hadn't been a ridiculously high commission....

"No problem." James looked at him intently. "You okay?"

"You know how I feel about him."

"I know." James was the only one who had a clue, truly his best friend at the agency. Another cat, who got how deeply they felt about potential mates and men they'd wronged.

"So I'm okay, but I'm not okay."

"Right." James plopped one hip on his desk. "What's the problem, exactly?"

"I can't trust myself." James had known him when he'd been with Mal. Brock had believed he and Mal were mates, had believed they were connected, and it had all been a lie.

A deadly lie.

It had taken almost a year to recover physically, and he was a fucking shifter.

The mental part....

"Yeah, but you obviously trust him."

"Yes." Griz was amazing, solid, tempting, and one hell of a friend.

Brock just wasn't ever going to let someone get so close he was compromised. Not ever again. Not even when he was getting to need Locke. A lot.

"Then see where it goes. You two... resonate." James waved a hand when he said the ridiculous new-age word.

"He makes me want to be stupid, Jimmy."

"Oh, honey, you never do anything impulsive." James patted his hand, which was clenched on his desk. "Damn, you're so tense." James grabbed his hand and started massaging.

Brock's eyes crossed. "Oh, why can't I be impulsive about you? You give the best hand massages." He and James had no sexual chemistry. None. Friendship? Yes. Brotherhood? Absolutely.

"Because a cat needs friends who just love him."

"Well, it's much appreciated, *amigo*."

"I know. So how is our new guy going to react if Mr. Wolfy takes a swing at him?"

"Mmm. Well...." Brock chuckled. "If Griz doesn't kill him and hide the body, he'll be fine. Calm."

"Neat. I can't wait."

"I have to admit, I'm curious to see how he takes to PI work." Most of the time Brock surprised himself with how well he took to it. Black ops had been easy for him, which probably said bad things about his character, but Mick tailored the work to everyone's skills.

"Bears are fascinating, because you think they're all goofy, and then suddenly they're amazeballs."

Nodding, he grinned at James. "Exactly. Locke is more... with it than Kit, but he's got a lot of the same traits."

"Kit's a baby. I sort of love that innocence." Jimmy grinned at him, eyebrows waggling.

"Oh, ew." Innocence didn't do it for him. He adored Kit, though. Thank God he wasn't trying to mate with the kid.

"Well, I don't want to fuck him, dork. I just like him."

"Oh, good. I would have to hurt you if you messed with him." Brock tilted his head. "Do you have a type, James?"

"All my sex is virtual, man. I'm a kitty waiting to get catfished."

"Uh-huh." That was a nonanswer, but Brock let it go. He wasn't one to talk about himself, so how could he yell at James?

"Besides, the boss keeps me busy, right?"

"He does. You're our anchor. And not in the dragging us into the deep sort of way." He reached up, stroked the deep scar on James's cheek. They matched a little now.

"Yeah." James smiled. "Well, I guess that's good, huh?"

"Yes." If Jimmy left, he would go.

"Well, if you need me, holler. Like to talk."

"We should groom soon, hmm?"

James paused, then grinned hugely. "We should. Oh, I would love that."

"I would too. Soon. This weekend?" Brock loved his cat time with his bestie, though he'd never admit it to anyone else.

"I'll be here."

"Cool." Brock stood, then bent to kiss James's cheek. "I need to go get pizza."

"Have fun! Take a chance!"

"I am." He muttered it, but headed up to the third floor where the lofts spread out for all of them.

Locke was waiting on the landing, file folder in hand, and Brock grinned at the big bear, nodded. "Hey, stranger."

"Hey. I like this building better than the last one," Locke deadpanned.

"Yeah, the last one had fallen down by the time you saw it."

"Right?" Locke winked.

"Come on in. We can order on the phone." His place was simple—sofa, TV, kitchenette, huge bed.

"Thanks. Comfy." Locke looked around, but the nose was the giveaway. It worked furiously.

"It is. Simple, warm, cozy." He needed to decorate. The walls had that barren, rental-house look, but the destruction of their last building had been pretty complete, and they'd been busy.

Damn busy.

"It is. I should paint you something." Locke chewed his lip, as if he'd said too much.

"I'd love that. I have all this wall space." He collapsed down on the sofa.

"Cool." Locke set the file aside on an end table before joining him in a sprawl. "Oh, this is nice. Why don't I have a couch?"

"This was my first purchase. Somewhere to flop."

"Yeah. I've been living out of a duffel bag." Locke toed off his shoes. "Is this okay? I want to put my feet up, but I don't want to offend."

"Suitcase traveling sucks. I'm not offended, Griz."

"Cool."

His feet had been all over at Locke's last house, so he guessed this wasn't any different. Brock leaned, smiling over at his friend. "How was your first day?"

"Good. James got me all sorts of virtual information, and Dylan and Carrie went over all the house rules."

"Ah yes. No biting without permission. No licking

without permission. No sniffing butts—that one was for Dylan back in the beginning."

"Well, I meant billing hours and expenses, but we touched on no scratching the furniture too." Now Locke was laughing at him. "Dylan is an uncontrolled sniffer, huh?"

"Was. He got better." He curled his legs up, facing Locke. "He still lives by his nose a lot."

"Ah. Yeah, a nose knows." Bears had an amazing sense of smell. Better than the big cats, better than wolves, even.

"What does your nose know?" Brock watched Locke, feeling warm and lazy in his skin.

"That you smell good." Locke sniffed some more. "That you spend more time on the bed than the couch, as much as you like it here."

"I do. I love my naps."

"You do." Locke moaned and stretched. "Oh, my back likes this."

"You...." *Don't do it. Don't. Don't offer.* "Where are you sleeping tonight?"

"Huh?" Locke carefully kept that face turned away from him. "Oh, I'm fine, man. I've got a place to go."

"Right." It all clicked. Locke was either living in his truck or staying at some fleabag motel. He'd just come back to town when Brock had called him, and clearly he hadn't bothered to get an apartment. Or he'd lost it. The house had been sold when their old team broke up, he knew.

"You know we'll be up late with the case and food. Beer. Stay with me?"

"Oh, yeah. Okay. That would work." Locke did look at him then. "Thank you. For real."

"Not a problem." And he meant it. Locke was welcome with him.

"Cool." Locke brightened. "Did you order yet?"

"I didn't. I want pepperoni and sausage and green olive. What about you?"

"Sausage and mushrooms and black olives?" Locke rubbed his belly, looking downright ecstatic.

"Mmm. And wings and garlic bread." That was a hungry bear, even after two sandwiches today, Brock could tell. "And cheesecake?"

Locke groaned. "Oh, hell yes. Please."

Brock grabbed his phone and ordered. "They'll call from downstairs when they get here."

"Yum." Locke sighed, wiggling his toes in his socks. "Tell me what I need to know about the team. Besides the butt sniffing."

"Kit is a sweetheart. He was an orphan—the pack took him in as a young adult. Good guy—he's sensitive, delicate. Well, except as a bear. Then? Not so much."

"He's goofy too. Fannish, right? I saw he had a Ravenclaw crest on his jacket. *Harry Potter.*"

How did Locke even know what this shit was?

"Impressive. Him and the fox? They're into that shit."

"Cool. I'm not, but I did a bodyguard stint for a kidnap target who was twelve. She was totally into assigning me my Hogwarts house." Locke's laugh made his belly hurt.

He wanted to climb into Locke's lap and rub.

Locke looked up, gaze locking with his. Yeah, he was probably throwing out all sorts of scent. This was crazy as hell, and so sudden to be falling back into, but he couldn't help it. He had needs and right now he needed Locke.

Scooting up, Locke moved toward him over the cushions, crawling a little. It should have been silly, but it was hot as hell.

"Griz...." His cock was hard as nails, his body aching. How could they go zero to sixty like this?

"Uh-huh. I—Brock." Locke got right up in his face and kissed him.

He wanted to yowl. Brock arched, their lips clinging. He lapped at Griz, begging entrance. Opening up, his bear let him in, moaning when he took that mouth. Heavy hands wrapped around him, dragging them together.

Brock undulated, his whole body alight in the best way. He had his fingers tangled in Griz's heavy hair, holding them together.

Griz just loved on him, slow and sure and solid. That body radiated heat. He ached for this bear; he needed to know everything about Locke again. It had been so long, and even then he'd pushed Griz away so fast.

Griz grabbed his ass and began to rock them, a slow, steady motion that made his eyes cross. He climbed into Griz's lap all the way, kneading those shoulder muscles with his fingers.

"Baby." Griz grunted for him, hands heavy around his hips.

"You're so tight. So stiff."

"I'm good. Right here." Griz just kissed him again, shutting them both right up.

He focused on digging in, helping those tight muscles ease.

"Oh." Griz rolled his head down, really tensing up for a moment before relaxing in a sudden rush.

"There. There, Griz. Right there." He hummed, purring with pleasure at being able to help.

"Uh-huh. Oh, thank you." Those muscles loosened for him, really letting go. Griz was.... Something was going on there.

"Welcome." He leaned in for another kiss, telling himself it wasn't his business.

"Mmm." The kiss went deeper than the last, Griz more demanding, and he opened up, letting Griz in. They traded the lead back and forth, laughing when they bumped noses.

When his phone rang, he groaned. "Pizza. Dammit."

"Right." Griz laughed, the sound husky and rough. "Should I go down?"

"Nah. I'll be kitty quick."

Griz patted his ass. "Should I get some drinks?"

"Beer's in the fridge."

"Excellent. You're a star, kitty."

"Meow." He laughed and bounced downstairs, heading for the front door. The pizza guy was standing there, and he opened the first set of doors and closed them behind him before opening the second. No endangering the team. They'd put in all sorts of fail-safes, and none of them were impenetrable, but this building was way more crocodile proof. Crocodile shifters. Jesus, he still couldn't believe they'd faced down those evil fuckers and lived.

"Order for Brock?"

"Yep." He had one hand on his back holster, just in case. "It's been paid for online. You can leave it on the chair there."

"Sure. Thanks." The guy slid the order onto the chair. "Uh, two pizzas, wings, and garlic loaf. Have a good night."

"Did you bring the cheesecake?"

"Oh! Yeah. It's in the separate bag there." The kid pointed. "So it didn't get hot."

"You rock. The tip's coming online. I won't stiff you."

"Thanks. Night."

Same protocol. He waited for the kid to go back out the main doors before letting himself in the second set. No bum-rushing.

Then he grabbed the food and bounded upstairs, bags in hand. The best way to a bear's heart was really his stomach.

Griz had pulled out two beers and two of his little plastic plates.

"Good deal." Brock smiled, laying everything out on the counter. "Come and get it."

"God, this smells amazing." Griz got himself a bit of every-thing, and Brock smiled. He did like to watch a man eat.

Especially this one.

He grabbed a couple of slices before heading back to the couch. He curled up with a purr and turned on some old-school samba.

"Oh, I like it." Griz munched on a piece of pizza.

"Thanks. It makes me happy." Music gave him joy. Most people wouldn't believe it, but it was true.

"I love the salsa stuff."

"Do you dance?" He'd never seen Griz dance.

"I do. Kind of like a bear at the circus, but I like it."

"Me too. A lot." Brock snapped up a chicken wing.

"Yeah?" Griz looked at him, head tilted.

"Sure. Moving is what I do, right?" Even with the scars and the occasional stiffness.

"You do. And you do it beautifully."

He flushed, his cheeks going red-hot. There was some-thing in Locke's eyes, a heat that made his heart stutter. "Thank you."

"I would dance with you anytime."

"We have room here."

"We do." Griz set his plate aside, springing up to offer him a hand.

He took it, knowing it wasn't the wisest thing to do, but he wanted it. He needed to dance. Somehow that exposed more of his soul than the earlier kisses.

Griz tugged him to the center of the room, then pulled him close, arms around him. The man was such a liar. There wasn't an ungraceful bone in his body.

The music changed to a slow rhumba, and Brock moaned and let all his tension out, pressing himself into the curves of Griz's body.

They swayed to the sensuous beat, Griz humming and

swinging him in a slow circle. He followed, one cheek on Griz's cheek.

They were floating, Griz perfectly in time with the music.

He couldn't remember when he'd had such a lovely time.

A lovely time? Listen to him.

This was dangerous. Caring. Letting people in. Tomorrow he would go back to work, but tonight he was going to let himself have this.

He loved to be held, to move his body with a lover.

That big body felt hot and right against his, and he loved Griz's voice when he buzzed softly.

He lifted his face and kissed Griz's jaw.

"Mmm." Griz dipped him, pecking a kiss on his lips.

"Perfect." He held on to those wide shoulders.

"Yeah?" Griz had a tiny bit of uncertainty in his expression. "Hit the happy spot?"

"Goddess, yes. I needed that."

"Me too." Griz laughed, pulling him back to his feet. So strong.

"Come finish eating, hmm? We have goodies."

"We do. Thank you." Griz moved with him, grabbing more food before moving back to the couch. He looked so happy.

That was perfect. Honestly. Griz deserved some joy. That hard tension in him just wasn't right.

Maybe they both deserved some.

Brock brought the cheesecake, along with two forks. They could share later.

"Yum. I like the garlic bread."

"It's got a nice crisp to it, hmm?"

"It does. And a lot of butter."

He grabbed a piece and dared to offer it to Griz, who nipped it out of his fingers. Griz closed his eyes and moaned happily. So pretty. Seriously. He fed Griz another bite.

"So good to me," Griz murmured.

"You're important." And that was the truth. *Deus*, he'd forgotten how much he liked this man, desired him.

"Thank you." That pleased flush was amazing.

"You're welcome." Anytime. He really meant it, even if nothing else came of it. He could deal if they were only friends.

He wanted to be something deeper. Brock just wasn't sure he knew how.

"Stop worrying, kit. We're simply enjoying one another."

He blinked at his bear. He was worrying. Kind of obsessively. "No. You're right."

Griz touched his hand, the contact soft but not tentative. "This is good."

"Uh-huh. Better than." He brought Griz's fingers to his lips.

Those dark eyes went heavy-lidded, Griz rumbling. Brock kissed one knuckle after another, taking his time, lingering on the fingertips.

"You have the most amazing mouth."

He could smell Griz's sudden increased desire on the air.

"Do I?" He wrapped his lips around Griz's trigger finger, tongue working at the tip.

"Oh. Yes. Oh, God." Griz's head fell back, his body rocking.

He let his eyes close, let himself focus and suck.

Griz was moaning continuously, his whole body moving, those eyes almost closed. He could see Griz in his mind's eye, almost glowing, as well. The big bear's aura was so clear and wondrous.

He moved near, crawling into Griz's lap.

Griz grabbed his ass, pulling him closer until not much air moved between them. "Kiss me."

He lifted his face, offering his lips. "Yes."

That kiss curled his toes. He'd had a lot of experience with sex, but less with making love. He thought this was more making love, because Griz treated him as if he was precious.

He was held close, but not tight, and Griz rocked him, hands sliding on his spine.

Brock arched up, rubbing like the cat he was. Wanting more.

Griz grabbed his ass and squeezed, and that made his feet draw up. He panted, his body starting to move in time with Griz.

"Good. God, Brock. You feel so good."

"You do too. *Por favor.*" This felt so big, and would get even better. Naked. Coming.

"Yes. Naked. Coming. Now, kitty."

"I—what did you say?" He sat up so he could tug off his shirt.

"Oh, fuck yes." Griz reached for him and pulled him in, lips wrapping around one of his nipples. He bucked, writhing at the sudden, wonderful pressure.

That growl made him bow his back and offer more. Everything. He was being a fool, but he was a happy fool.

Griz swooped back up and kissed him until he was dizzy, stealing his breath.

He craved more, had to have Griz's skin, so he tugged the bear's shirt off. Griz helped, then undid the button of the "tactical but somehow decently dressy for interview day" pants.

The ridge of that heavy cock made his eyes cross. Oh.

"Uhn. More." Griz pressed up against his touch.

"Yes. Look at you." His fingers curled around Griz, stroking him, base to tip.

"Rather look at you." Griz rocked for him, though.

He wasn't going to argue. They were touching and learning, and he needed it.

Brock was just gonna go with it for now.

———

Locke was pretty sure he'd hit his head and was in a dream world where everything was perfect and amazing. He didn't want to wake up.

He didn't intend to. Brock was touching him, stroking him off, giving him what he desired.

He was going to soak it all in, to experience every moment.

"*Alegre*," Brock purred. "I could ride you like a prized pony."

"Okay. Yes. Anything." *Please.* In fact, there was nothing he desired more.

"Yeah?" Brock raised his eyebrows. "I will."

"Then let's do it."

"Come to bed. There's no reason to act like this isn't worth sharing."

"Mmm. Yes." He took Brock's hand, then stood, tugging his lover along. His lover. Oh, that was a hopeful phrase.

The bed was huge and welcoming, and the scent was all Brock, making him growl softly. His body tightened even more, and Locke thought he might be hard-pressed to control himself. Then Brock began to strip down, baring that scarred body to him.

He licked his lips. God, he loved how Brock looked. Loved it.

Brock watched him closely, and he let himself admire, let Brock see. He knew how it felt to be uncertain, to worry, and there was nothing for Brock to be worried about. Those scars were maps of strength.

"I want to touch, to trace every line." His fingers actually twitched.

"I hate them."

"I'll show you how to love them." He reached out and

found one line, touching it and dragging along the twisting mark.

Brock shuddered as if he'd hit the man, but Locke was going to do this. He was going to teach Brock to take this back. He was going to love his mate, dammit.

Locke would admit it, if only to himself. How Brock shut him out, he had no idea. But he knew the truth.

He knew and he could have faith. Now.

Fingers wandering, Locke traced another scar, then another. *Come on, love. Feel this.*

Brock grabbed his wrist, holding his hand against that warm skin. "You're going to make me go too early."

"I don't want that. I want you to get me all wet and ride me."

"Fuck yes. Now. Now is good. Get naked."

Locke stripped down the rest of the way, the expression in those green eyes stunning and lovely, urging him on.

Brock licked his lips again and grabbed the lube from the nightstand before yanking down the covers, releasing another rush of scent.

Jerking, Griz panted, his whole body overheated.

They climbed into the sheets, both naked and needing to touch. He reached for Brock again, and the man came right to him, meeting him fully. They kissed, the heat rising up as they rubbed along each other.

Goddess, this was real. This was his Brock.

He moaned, his head spinning. So long. It had been so long.

"I have you." Brock's hand was slick as it dragged over his cock.

"Yep." All he could do was nod and grunt, because with Brock's hand on his dick, his brain stopped working.

"I need you." That callused thumb rubbed his slit.

"Uh-huh. Right here. Hard and ready." He moved to his back and stroked his cock, proving how ready he was.

Brock stopped and stared, eyes focused on him with laser precision. Griz's nostrils flared, and he spread his legs, making an offer.

Nodding, Brock slid over top of him, rubbing their cocks together. "I'm aching for you."

"You going to ride me or fuck me, baby?" He would take either. With pleasure.

"I'm going to ride you into the ground."

"Well, get my fingers wet so I can get you ready."

Brock grabbed his hand and took two fingers, sucking them in with a slurp.

He waited, watching again, because he could handle that all night. Well, except he required Brock on his cock. He wanted to stretch Brock wide, make him moan.

Locke knew he was the man for that job. God, he could make Brock fly. He pulled his wet fingers free, hoping to open Brock up.

He didn't hesitate; he pushed his fingers behind Brock's heavy, fuzzy balls, searching for that tiny hole.

Brock bent, spreading. He offered, and Locke took, pushing in two fingers, gasping at the tight heat. Goddess, that was perfect.

"So tight, baby. Gonna feel so good around me."

"Been a long time since I trusted anyone."

Locke nodded. "But you can trust me."

"I do. You are my friend."

"I am." He loved Brock. So bad. But he would never betray the trust Brock put in him by pushing that agenda. He pressed deeper, curling his fingers and petting Brock inside.

"Uhn!" Brock rolled up, then stretched back out. "More."

Oh, that made his mouth dry. He gripped and repeated the touch, watching Brock move on his hand. His cat was dancing for him. Locke leaned closer and took a kiss, fucking Brock's lips in time with his fingers inside that sweet, hot ass.

Brock wrapped around him, arms about his neck. "Please, Griz. Now. I need it."

"I got you." Brock had never been scared of a little burn, so he withdrew his fingers, his cock still slick from Brock's touch. Brock grabbed him with one hard hand, rocking back on him and taking the tip of him in.

Locke gritted his teeth, pulling tight with his belly muscles to keep him where he was. He wanted to start thrusting, but Brock had to set the pace. Brock rippled, taking him in, inch by inch by inch.

"That's it, baby. Oh, so hot. Yeah." He encouraged Brock on, his voice a low growl.

"Thick fucking prick." Brock yowled for him.

Brock arched, that tight body bending so Locke could slide the final inch he needed. He held Brock's hips, hands draped around that silky, soft skin. Despite the scars, everything about Brock was fluid and slinky and gorgeous.

And his.

He hid the thought, but he meant it.

Brock's eyes went wide, that body shuddering, Brock's muscles clamping down around him. Yes. Yes, Brock heard him. He almost started to crow. He didn't, but he'd known it. His mate.

He began to pull Brock down onto him, over and over.

Brock bounced, growling, eyes glowing this crazy green.

He held Brock's gaze, accepting the wild energy, the need. Locke would take everything Brock had to give and pass it back tenfold.

Brock yowled softly, and his mate arched on his dick.

"Yes. That's it, baby. Look at your cock. So hard." He slapped at it a little.

Brock's teeth snapped together, hunger flooding him. He

felt it! He felt Brock's desire, a bond between them opening up, one he always knew could be there. "My kit," he growled. "Mine."

"Griz!"

Brock was losing it, unraveling a bit at a time, but that was okay. Locke had him.

Right there, on top of him. In his hand, when he gripped Brock's cock. Brock bowed fiercely, humping down on him.

They were cooking with oil now, moving fast, and he kept one hand on Brock's dick, one on his hip, yanking.

"Soon. Soon, Griz. Make me come."

"I will. I swear. Want to come with you." He wanted it all.

All Brock could do was nod at him, stare.

Locke panted, his chest heaving, his cock swelling even more. He turned them, driving down into Brock, fucking him good and hard.

Crying out, Brock dug both hands into his shoulders, holding on tight.

"Come on, baby. Come on my cock." He demanded it, tugging maybe too hard on that sweet prick. The pleasure flooded him, the rush of hunger from his mate nearly unbearable.

Letting himself be swept along for the ride, Locke came hard, Brock's muscles milking him hard as they flew. The scent of Brock's seed was perfect, filling his senses.

He turned them both again, staying buried deep inside. He closed his eyes once Brock slumped on his chest, his whole body alight but his mind at peace.

"Stay." It was a quiet request.

"Yes. Oh, yes." Not just because he was tired of not having a place to stay....

"No. Because this is good."

He beamed. *Yes. Yes, because this is good.* "Very good."

Brock began to laugh. "Good good good good."

He had to join in, all but rolling on the bed. He felt the same sense of relief and joy that emanated from his new lover.

Brock held his face between his hands, playing with him.

Such a kitty. Always with the paws.

He scooped Brock close, devouring his mouth before pulling back. "Cheesecake?"

"Yes. Oh." Brock's eyes went wide. "I forgot. Yum. I'll grab it."

That gave him a lovely view, all the way to the coffee table. And back.

Hello. God, Brock was gorgeous, making his mouth dry.

Then his own personal wet dream crawled on the mattress, holding a cheesecake. It was like the best kind of porn, and he inhaled deep, imprinting hard.

Brock snuggled right up against him, then handed him a fork.

THREE

B rock slept hard enough that he woke up hungover and dizzy, confused and headachy. He tried to lift his head, growling softly at the throb. *Oh. Oh, fuck.*

"Baby?" The voice in his head didn't help at all.

"My head...."

Huge hands circled his skull, and the pain disappeared with a pop.

"Oh." Brock closed his eyes for a moment. "Morning, Paddy."

"Locke. There. Good morning." Those hands were magic. Pure fucking heaven.

"Mmm." He all but purred, curling into that big body for its warmth. Griz smelled heavenly, musky and rich, and he clung.

Sweet, giant bear. Surely they could stay here for a few minutes.

A couple hours.

A week or so.

Then he would get back to real life. One of them would do a stakeout, and they would drift....

He reached up and stroked Griz's heavy mass of dark hair.

"Mmm. Hey," Griz rumbled. That belly rumbled not too far from his ear. "Uh. Do you have stuff to cook?"

"Eggs. Sausage. Cheese. Uh. Eggs." He liked eggs.

"I like eggs. Better than smoked salmon."

"Mmm... I like that. And tuna. Coffee with heavy cream." Brock's eyes crossed.

"Croissants with berries. Hash browns with bacon in them."

They were having breakfast sex.

"Waffles with butter in every little hole."

"Yes. Okay. Do you have a waffle iron?" Griz surged up, holding on so he didn't plop down.

"I don't know. I bet Kit has one in the big kitchen. I can ask."

"Cool. I'll start gathering stuff."

He leaned and reached, scrabbling for his phone. Kit was fourth down on speed dial.

"'Lo?" Kit sounded a little snuffly. Not awake.

"Waffle iron?"

"Uh.... Yeah. I mean, I have one."

"Can I borrow it? We'll make you waffles."

"We?" Amusement crept into Kit's voice.

"Me and Griz."

"Griz?"

"Locke. I need the waffle iron, Kit."

"I just woke up! Gimme ten minutes."

"Make it five and we'll add bacon." He hung up, knowing Kit would take that offer.

"You drive a hard bargain, kitty." Griz's rumble was pure happiness.

"I do. I want those waffles." Sadly, Griz had pulled on pants. The view was... yeah. Still good. "I haven't had waffles in a long time. I like to crunch."

"Right. Dark crispy waffles." Griz grinned when a knock sounded. "Waffle iron."

"I'll grab it." He tugged on a pair of shorts and bounced to the door. "Hey, Kit!"

"Hey, grumpy cat." Kit rubbed cheeks with him. "Waffle iron. Am I staying for breakfast, or are you delivering?"

"I'm going to feed him in bed, little bear."

"Oh!" Kit's face flushed, and he thrust the waffle maker at Brock. "Gotcha."

"I'll bring you some later."

"Uh-huh. Whatever. Going back to bed. Pervs." Kit waved and headed back toward his place.

Brock locked up before moving to present his prize to Griz. "Ta-da."

He got a kiss for his efforts, and he swore he could feel Griz all inside him. Brock wanted to run, but just as much, he wanted to stay and bask in Griz's sunbeam.

Besides. Waffles.

He curled up on the bed, answering emails on his laptop and keeping one eye on Griz.

Griz had put music on his Echo and was shaking it to a Motown classic. Look at that. He liked it. He could lick that sweet lower back and make Griz scream.

Griz glanced at him over one shoulder, eyes dark. "I can feel you."

"Can you?" He didn't know what to think about that.

"I can. It's so cool." Griz beamed. "It's like a hum at the base of my skull."

"A hum, huh?"

"Yeah. And it gets louder when you stare at my butt." Griz wiggled it again, giving him a show.

"You have a fine ass. It needs biting."

"Anytime. Well, maybe not now. Since there's waffle irons and bacon grease."

"Right. Exceptional point." Although he could kneel back there and spread Griz with his thumbs and....

"Brock!"

"Mmmm." There were advantages to the mind-meld thing, huh?

Weirdnesses too, and he wasn't sure what to do, but still... no one had ever accused him of not biting when he could. He liked it, in fact....

"I could bite you, kit. We will tear each other up."

"We will. After breakfast," he teased. "You promised me good food, remember."

"I did. I will." Griz was sounding a wee bit confused. It was adorable. Maybe Locke was as uncertain about all this as he was.

"You're all right, bear. *Respira*."

"I am. Bacon. Waffles." Griz went back to cooking, slinging bacon like a pro.

"Bacon. Waffles. Syrup. Butter."

"Do you have syrup?" Griz looked worried suddenly.

"I do. In the fridge. I've been having it over biscuits."

"Oh, good. Okay. I know you have butter." Griz chuckled. "Great for hair balls."

"I will bite you, bear."

"You keep promising." Griz pulled out a perfect, crispy, dark gold waffle.

"I do. I'm good that way."

"I can't wait." Griz gave him this look that damn near burned him to the ground.

He found himself up and moving, eyes fastened on Griz.

"Mmm." Griz set the bacon off the burner, then reached for him.

Brock couldn't stay away. He needed this touch.

Griz grabbed him, kissing his lips and hugging him. "I like breakfast with you."

Yeah. Yeah, so did he. With Griz. Together. Happy. Not that happy was an easy word for Brock.

They danced a bit, but the waffle iron dinged again, so Griz moved about to take things out of pans and irons.

Brock grabbed plates and butter, orange juice, and syrup.

They would have breakfast in bed for sure.

Griz put a bunch of waffle batter in the fridge. "I'll make more for Kit. After."

"Mmm. Yeah. Kit will go back to bed for a while."

"Don't worry about the little bear. Worry about the one in *your* bed."

"*Oh, naughty Griz.*" Brock laughed, his heart hammering. Waffles shouldn't cause such happiness.

"*Naughty.*" The thought buzzed through him.

He poured syrup on the waffles after Griz smeared butter in every hole, as promised.

They curled together on the bed, feeding each other, stealing long, lazy kisses in between bites. Sticky and sweet, the syrup was a perfect counterpoint to the crunchy, salty bacon and delicate, crispy waffle. God, he was in heaven.

Griz squeezed his ass and rumbled his agreement. That was a happy bear. So much better than the sad, tired bear from yesterday. It occurred to him to ask about that, but he refused to spoil the mood.

He leaned into Griz's throat, humming and lapping gently, sharing their scent.

"Mmm." Griz put a hand behind his head, holding him there. He could accept that. He nuzzled in with a deep moan, the scent of male need like a drug.

He wanted more. Food was done. Time to connect.

"*Time to fuck.*"

The thought was rough, raw, and filled him in a rush. "*Yes. Yes.*" He thought it was just that time.

He straddled Griz's lap, their cocks rocking and rubbing together, and when he knelt up tall, that heavy club of a prick slid behind his balls, teasing him.

"Mmm. Slinky, gorgeous kitty."

"Need you. Everywhere." Every inch.

"You got me." Griz was all over him, touching and kissing. The bites made his eyes roll, made him buck a bit.

Griz was a fucking force of nature. A storm he could revel in. Griz's cock nudged his hole again, begging entrance, and he bore down.

He was still plenty open, if not wet. He didn't mind the burn at all. Brock got off on it, in fact.

"I know. I can feel it."

"Stop reading my mind and fuck me." Brock snarled a little, because he felt too vulnerable.

"Easy, love. Easy." Griz pushed him over and drove in, making him scream in pleasure.

No, there was nothing easy about this. Griz was going to give him the pounding he needed.

He arched and bucked under Griz, loving the way Griz covered him. That big body was so strong, so heavy. Griz surrounded him with scent too, so dark and good. He rubbed, body undulating under all those heavy muscles.

"Sweet kit." Griz had rolled him, so when Griz slammed down, he wrapped his legs around the man, dragging him in deeper, closer.

"Fuck, you're strong. I want you so bad." Griz bared his teeth.

"You have me."

Those black eyes flared. "I do. I most certainly do."

Brock actually lifted his chin to let Griz bite. Yeah, he had a rep as a badass, and he was. But he had to have this. His lover.

Griz roared, the sound huge, vibrating the building itself. The noise held joy, triumph, and perhaps a hint of worry, and Brock understood completely. He couldn't stop this. He needed it. He needed Griz.

"More." Griz slammed into him hard enough to rock the bed, a plate falling off onto the floor.

"Everything." He dragged his nails up over Griz's back.

Griz grunted, eyes dropping half closed.

"Mine." He wanted to make sure Griz heard it.

"Yours. Yes. I so am." Griz rocked him, really pounding. He swore he could feel Griz's cock all the way inside him, deep in his throat.

The man was freaking huge and so hard for him, and he took every inch with one happy cry after another. He was flying, just fucking soaring, his Griz lighting a fire along his nerves.

Griz pushed up, watching him, dark eyes burning down on him.

Brock snapped his teeth at Griz, missing that wide shoulder by a fraction.

"Mine." Griz snapped right back. "Bite. Please."

Okay, he had permission. Time to get toothy. He pressed up, teeth sinking into Griz's shoulder.

Griz shouted, banging into him, right against his gland inside. Brock screamed around the flesh in his teeth, his entire body drawing tight.

When Griz came into him, that was all it took. Brock shot as well, his body convulsing.

For a long, long moment, the universe expanded infinitely, huge and scary, then tightened down to the two of them.

Then they slumped down on the bed, and he thought there might be a waffle under his elbow. Someone would eat it. Maybe. Later.

Right now he just wanted to snuggle. Bears were the best at that.

His bear growled, nosing his temple. *"Sleep."*

"Yes, bear. Sleep. Don't forget Kit's waffles."

"In an hour or so." Griz patted his hip.

That touch was all he needed to sink into sleep.

Griz slipped out of bed after that hour or so. He had waffles to make, and he knew they both had to get to work.

He was feeling amazing. Amazing. Even if he did have to peel waffles off the bed and wipe up a syrup spill.

Brock had given himself to Locke, just offered himself right over. He was simply humbled. Right back in the love he'd always had.

His kit was scarred and heartsore, but Griz intended to heal and protect and love Brock and make it better.

Now, he would bet when Brock woke up this time, his kitty was going to be grumpy. Running a little scared.

There would be snarling and chest bumping, and it would be fine, because it was his kitty.

His. Brock had said so.

He'd been rewarded for his long years of patience, and he could hear it, buzzing along his spine.

Brock's mind was quiet, the need for sleep obviously plaguing him.

"Easy, baby. You're good. I have you."

Brock mumbled, but didn't wake. *"Sweet love."* Okay. Only he would call Brock sweet.

Locke began to cook again, the view of his mate curled in the sheets the best thing ever. The sun was shining, he had a place to rest his head, life was good. The very thought was such a lovely surprise compared to his recent life.

Bacon went into the oven this time because that would

smell less, and he churned out waffles, knowing he would share with all the guys.

When the waffles started getting done, he put on his pants, covered Brock up completely, and texted Kit and Mick.

Kit knocked softly a few minutes later. "You need any help?" he asked when Griz opened the door.

"Please," he whispered back. "Brock's worn."

"Understood." Kit crept in, taking plates of waffles and bacon out. They would all go to the main lounge, he was sure.

"Enjoy, little bear."

"Oh, I will. Thank you." Kit waved.

Griz assumed they had butter and syrup downstairs. Kit hadn't asked. That was okay. He'd save a few waffles for their next meal. He went to the couch to grab his laptop. Might as well work and admire Brock as much as he could. As soon as he returned to the bed, he had a warm man in his lap, wrapped around him.

"Hey, kitty." He set the laptop aside, pulling Brock into his arms.

Brock was slinky and soft, hiding his claws for now.

He stroked Brock's back. "I could read to you, if you want. My Kindle is in the laptop bag." That would put Brock right back to sleep.

The soft purr filled the air, the agreement making him smile.

"Cool." He freed one arm, opening up the bag with that hand so he could pull out his lightweight Kindle, a gift from his mom. She loved that he still loved to read, even if they were, on occasion, strained.

He began to read aloud, and Brock melted into him, offering him a rush of peace, pleasure.

Soon, Brock was breathing deeply again, and he was reading silently but sharing the story with his mate. He petted as he read, utterly entranced. He loved that smooth skin, marred in spots by scars, but not ruined. No, those patches of ropy scar fascinated his fingers.

"Ugly."

"No, love. Not one bit. I love all of your skin. This means you're a survivor." For a shifter to scar, the wound had to be grievous.

"I thought he loved me."

A soft growl bubbled inside him, but he didn't let it out. Bastard fox. He stroked Brock's hair. *"Maybe he did. It doesn't matter now."*

No one would harm his kit again without paying for it. He would rip off heads and shit down necks.

Finally, Brock crawled up in his lap and started checking emails.

He grinned. That was his laptop. Kitty fantastico.

"We're going to have to deal with the asshole. We being you."

Griz nodded. He wasn't worried. Even Brock's eye was barely bruised now.

"I can do it. His wife is having multiple affairs. That's all he wanted to know, yeah?" Griz was better with people than Brock.

"Yeah. Mick should have chosen another investigator, eh? He doesn't love the felines."

"I guess you have to play a little Tetris when you're the boss."

"A little. Dylan's on a job with a corporate spy. Cool stuff."

"No shit? How did the wolf get that one?"

"He's collaborative, and he has Mr. Fox in his back pocket."

"Ah. And Mr. Fox is an information guy, right?"

Brock nodded. "I think he's half ferret."

"You ever met a ferret shifter?"

"They let Kit deal with the non-Apex folks. I have a tendency to nibble on anything smaller than a bobcat."

"The beavers are safe with you here?" The workers were still pounding away.

"What did James tell you?"

"About what?" Griz blinked, trying to change gears.

"The beavers." That smile was wicked.

"Oh! Uh, that they didn't hang out at night. Now I know why." Griz teased right back now that he knew what was what.

He could almost see Brock's long tail twitching.

"They're very industrious."

"Totally. Love their little hard hats."

He had to laugh out loud. The image of beavers in animal form wearing mini hard hats just tickled him.

Brock's grin made him take a kiss, opening that wicked mouth up. The flavor of his lover was better than any waffle or syrup.

The jolt of Brock's pleasure made him smile.

They kissed long and hard, deep touches that made him moan.

Brock's phone rang, "It's Raining Men" sounding.

He pulled back to stare. *What the hell?*

"Mick. Ignore it. Please."

"Oh. Okay." Should they ignore the boss? Were they supposed to be at work?

"Good choice."

The ring came again.

"Why is he calling you, kitty?"

"He wants *trabalho* or something. Doesn't he know I'm busy?"

"Nope. I mean, I told him there were waffles." That should earn them an hour.

"Kit took them down. I heard. I need to suck you. I'm busy."

"You want to, I'm so in." Oh, Locke was so, so in. That mouth could inspire him to write poetry. Well, except he was a visual artist. Not an artist, he guessed. He painted shit.

"I want to." Brock wriggled down, lips wrapping around Griz's cock as Griz's phone started to ring.

Nope. He'd washed up before he'd made the second batch of waffles, Brock was sucking him, and he was not going to miss a second of them. Mick could wait.

Brock wiggled as he sucked, ass wagging side-to-side, dark head bobbing in his lap, the suction around his cock like a Hoover.

His eyes rolled back in his head. So not grumpy kitty; this was a happy Brock. So much better than he'd expected.

He would remember this. His pussy cat liked a fat cock stretching his lips. Griz would make sure his was the only one to do it again. Possessive. That he could do.

Rolling his hips, he took Brock's mouth, ignoring it when both phones began to ring.

Brock grinned around his prick, tongue lashing the shaft.

Fuck. Oh, fuck, that was good. Evil man.

He dropped one hand to the top of Brock's head and rocked up. "So good."

"Mmmm." Brock's moan made his balls vibrate, and his toes curled.

Okay. Okay, no one had told him that he'd been missing that mouth. No one. He had been, though. So much. Brock was all over him, around him, scent and touch and hot, wet suction.

"I should have come here for you sooner. Gods, kit. Your mouth."

Brock cupped a hand under his balls, pressing up gently in reply.

He groaned, leaning back on his elbows so he could watch.

Griz wanted this to go on and on, even when the knocking started the door.

"You two can't stay in there all day!" Mick roared from the hallway.

Brock just sucked harder.

"We're busy!" he shouted back. "Really, very busy!"

Incredibly. Brock took him in to the root.

He grunted, his whole body arching to get more.

Brock rolled his balls again and tugged them, making his eyes cross again. He was going to go off like a rocket any minute.

There was something evil about burying yourself in your mate's mouth with your boss breathing on the door. His mate....

He laughed, letting his head fall back. Lord have mercy. He was a bad, bad man.

Brock scraped him a tiny bit with those teeth, and Griz rose back up, shouting, "Brock! Sweet!"

Griz bucked into Brock's throat.

Humming, Brock swallowed around him seconds later, pushing him hard, his balls drawing tight.

That was all he could take. Griz gave it up, coming hard.

Too soon Brock popped off his cock, kissed the tip of his prick. "Pants. We have to."

"No." He yanked Brock against him, grabbing that rigid dick.

Brock's eyes lit bright. "No?"

Oh, that felt good, that surprise and glorious pleasure.

"No. I want you to come." Locke stroked, starting a strong rhythm.

"Griz." Brock held him, eyes wide and wondering.

"Yes, baby. Yes." Griz pulled and tugged, focused on his mate, on his pleasure.

Brock was his, all the way, sensual and sexual and so fine.

That lean body twisted against him, Brock driving into his touch. Begging.

"Come on. Let me have you. Let me smell you."

Brock's cry was wild, fierce, ringing out. The next moment Brock was shooting for him, wet and hot, slick on his wrist and chest and belly.

"There. There, good. Gods, yes." Griz brought his hand up to his mouth, licking himself clean. His mate. This was his mate.

Brock's dazed eyes met his. "Wow."

Another knock sounded, this one softer. "Guys? Mick wants to see you."

"Okay, Kit. Just a second, huh? I'll be right down. Swear." Brock had baby-head.

"Got it. Thanks for the waffles!" Kit trundled off, his footsteps clomping.

Brock grinned up at him. "God, this is fun."

"It is." Griz kissed the tip of Brock's nose. "Time to face the music."

"We'll grin and apologize, and he'll send us to do surveillance."

"I like a stakeout. Unlike some grumpy kitties." Look at that. He'd put that smile on Brock's face.

"I might like it, if I can play with you."

"I bet you would. I bet you'd try to distract me." When he moved to wash up, Brock stopped him.

"Let Mick smell us."

"Evil cat."

Brock's grin was slow, easy, and absolutely glorious. "Yes, my bear."

"Come on, then." He grabbed pants, a T-shirt from his bag, and then his shoes. He would change once he knew what Mick's punishment was.

Brock dressed in his usual all-black, complete with hoodie. "Let's go listen to the boss bark."

"Look at you. An ink blot from juvenile delinquent land."

"It's a great look for me, isn't it?"

"It so is." He ran a hand over that fine ass when it passed him.

"Thanks." Brock grinned up at him, green eyes dancing.

"Anytime, baby. Anytime."

Time to face the music, indeed.

FOUR

ick was foaming. Like for real. Foaming.

It was funny as fuck. Brock was happy, well-fucked, and three orgasms in over just twelve hours.

So he was in a damn good mood and willing to ignore Mick's shouting.

"You're not listening."

"You noticed."

"I did."

"I'm trying to be good and let him vent." Brock grinned. *"It's really our only option. He'll wear himself out eventually."*

Griz smiled back at him. "Mick? What are we going to need to do to make it up to you?"

"Remember this is not a whore house!"

"Hey!" Brock snapped. "I fucking pay rent. If I want to fuck every motherfucking second I'm in my apartment, that's none of your goddamn business."

Locke sat there, gone very still, and Brock knew that stony face. Not good.

Mick glared, and Brock bared his teeth. "Remember, boss, I am not bound by pack law. I'm here willingly."

"Yeah, yeah. Sorry if I overstepped." Mick said it to Locke, though. Bears. They were the biggest of the big predators. Everyone deferred to a grizzly.

"Sorry about not answering the phone, boss. The mating call hit hard. We were...."

"Busy," Brock finished.

"Yeah." Mick's ears went red. "Everyone in this goddamn place is mating up."

"I'm not going to apologize." He wouldn't hurt his bear like that. He wasn't sure what the fuck was actually happening, or if mating was going on, but he knew that.

Griz reached for his hand, took it, and held tight. That small smile was worth anything.

"Yeah, it just makes me as grumpy as you usually are. All the pheromones." Mick waved a hand. "Forget the cheating wife. I have a better job for the two of you."

"The two of us?" That sounded good. "What job?"

"Mostly surveillance. There's a warehouse that the client owns. He thinks it's being used, and right now he wants it to be a tax shelter. But it's not squatters. Thinks maybe someone is using it for some nefarious shit."

"Oh?" Brock could get up and install cameras. It wouldn't take much to slide in.

"Yeah. He wants discreet watching. Both digital and personal. Recording times and dates of deliveries. I was going to tell him we were too shorthanded, but since he's backed off about Brock and the hitting...."

"I'll do the cameras, boss. No problem. He just wants intel, no interaction?"

"Nothing yet. We'll see from there. Take different cars."

At least the crocs hadn't killed their fleet. SUVs they still had.

"That doesn't seem too fun, separating us."

Locke raised a brow. *"I think he means each time we go."* He turned to face Mick. "Right, Mick? We go together? We just take a different car each time."

Mick rolled his eyes. "God, now you're doing the mind meld like Rey and Dylan. Yes. That's it."

"Oops. Sorry." He grinned at Locke. "My bad."

Griz rolled his eyes as well, but they were just laughing.

"Out. Get out. Evil cat." Mick was laughing too, teeth bared.

"Going. Email me the deets."

"James will," Mick called as they left.

"I need to get to the storage room and dig out cameras." Brock would get some parabolic mics and some long-range lenses too.

"Sure. I need to get some shit out of my car. I'll meet you in the office?"

"Fair enough." He stole a kiss before he headed for James, a spring in his step.

———

"Come on. Oh my Gods. Tell me." James took his hand.

"My bear." What else could he say? Brock was so damn ashamed about pushing Griz away, thinking a fox was... what? More fashionable? No, he wasn't that much of an ass. He'd just been too young to believe in mate bonds when he and Griz had started out.

"Yay. Does it feel good?"

"It does." It felt like coming home.

"Excellent. That makes me happy. Is the sex amazing?"

His cheeks heated. He never blushed, but here he was.

James bounced. "Yeah? Fucking A."

"I know." Brock chuckled. "Keeping him."

"Good. You're needing CCTV?"

"I am. Something supersecret spy camera. Apparently these guys are doing a sneaky and they know it."

"Oh, those are the most fun." James moved back into the storeroom to dig through bins and baskets filled with glorious, random crap.

He couldn't believe how much James had salvaged from their destroyed headquarters. "All this shit still works?"

"Yep. The crocs weren't interested in equipment, just people."

"Yeah. Nice." He chuckled. "They weren't interested in thinking."

"I don't know that they could. Scary."

"No shit." Brock wasn't worried about too many predators, but those guys had been single-minded. Hell, they'd taken down an entire goddamn building.

James poked him, making him jump. "Box of tiny cameras."

"You've got the info to get them online?"

"Don't insult me, butthead." James looked down that stubby nose.

"Sorry, sorry, O Master of All Things Electronic."

"That's right. I got all I need; you get them all up." James touched his arm. "I'm so pleased for you."

He leaned in, then rubbed their cheeks together. "Thank you, friend."

"Okay. Is Locke going to need any parabolic mics or cameras?"

"I thought I would check him out both, just in case."

"You got it." James loaded stuff into a laptop.

Before long, Brock had two huge bags of electronics that he stuffed into the back of the SUV, carrying them to the office.

Locke came rumbling into sight, carrying a bag and a small cooler. "Snacks. Recorder, notebooks."

"Decent music?"

"You know it."

He and Griz shared a sneaking love for Latin pop, from Shakira to Enrique Iglesias.

He was excited—more excited than he'd ever been for a surveillance job. He accused Mick of punishing them with this, but he knew better. The boss was being kind, letting him and Griz settle their bond again.

"Relax, kitty. You're flying."

"I am." He couldn't help it. Brock didn't love being grumpy like the guys thought. It was just his natural state of being.

And he'd been raw, missing his lover, knowing he was wearing the scars of someone else. That was— No. Now was for Griz. Not the ex.

"Fuck the ex. You're mine."

"I am." Raw emotion flooded him. God, he wanted more of Griz. He wanted to dive into Griz's arms and hide there.

Of course, they had work to do, or Mick would fire them both....

"Come on. We'll have something wonderful to eat on stakeout."

Brock blushed, pleased down to the bone. He took Griz's hand, heading out to the big SUV he'd picked for today.

"So, we'll go, surveille, and I'll go after dark and wiggle in, hmm?"

"Carefully," Griz agreed.

"Carefully. Always."

"Mm-hmm." Griz didn't sound all that convinced.

"I mean it." Brock had a reason to be good. To do his job but not be reckless.

"Good. Because it would break me to lose you now."

He stared into Griz's dark eyes, then nodded. "I hear you."

For a second, the world stopped, went on without them. This was what he'd never felt with Mal, which had been purely physical. And maybe a bit of a glamour.

Griz growled softly, and he was wrapped in his mate. The smell of bear came to him, strong and musky. Griz was fighting not to shift.

Oh. Grooming. "Bear, please." They wouldn't fit in the SUV as animals, and they had to work.

"I know. Later, I promise. I need to.... I'll get us going." Griz let him go, clearly reluctant.

"Right. Us. Working."

"We have to." Griz chuckled, a low, pained sound.

"No, I know. I know. It's not fair."

"But it's money. And it brought me back to you." Locke got the car going, typing their locale into GPS with one hand.

"We're going to have to do other things than fuck during the night, you know."

"Like snuggling and grooming and eating?"

"Mmm." Oh, Griz made him purr with all of those suggestions.

"See? You didn't mean working. I know it." Griz reached over to squeeze his leg.

"I've been working for years. I want to play."

"Me too. Movies. Sushi."

"Sushi.... Spicy tuna?"

"Uhn." His bear smacked those luscious lips. "Salmon Philly."

"I approve. I like a nice scallop too."

"I even like eel." Griz was sounding hungry.

"Tempura? You like to crunch?"

"I do. Oh, we should go tomorrow." Griz bounced.

"I'm in. Can we share? There's a place with private rooms. I can feed you."

"Oh." Griz stopped bouncing, his hands clenching on the wheel. "Yes, please."

"I'll call for a reservation for two."

"Okay. I'll try not to come in my pants."

"I'll make sure to suck you off between courses." He loved teasing his bear.

"Wow. I'll order lots."

He laughed, just the barest bit overjoyed. Maybe a lot. Griz made him laugh so much.

"That's how it's supposed to be, mate. We're supposed to be happy."

"Dylan and Rey taught me that." He'd truly believed mating was about drama, and he had disappointed Griz.

"You were hurt, baby. Deep. If I ever see him...."

"If you ever see him, you leave him to me and you run." Mal wasn't only violent; he was evil. Psychotic.

"I'll do something." Griz bared his teeth. "I make no promises."

He wanted to rub, to purr, to luxuriate in this new, wonderful emotion.

Griz merged onto the highway at the command of the electronic voice. He cleared his throat. "What do we know about this case?"

"The client is the same guy who clocked me. Owns an import/export shop, and this warehouse is supposed to be empty. There's been activity, though, and Mr. Hetrick thinks it's someone honing in on his business."

"Gumpy nutpants. Anyone who would clock you is crazy. What does Mick think?"

"That this is a way to keep us busy. He thinks Hetrick is a paranoid freak who believes everyone is cheating him or cheating on him, but is willing to spend money. Which is why he pulled us off the wife and put us on this. Less sleazy."

"Ah. And together. That's decent of him. Why is he so sad?"

"He's got a weird little pack and no mate, I think."

"Ah. Well, he'll find the one." Griz truly believed it too. His mate had never lost hope, Brock thought.

"He will, and we'll discover who's in this warehouse."

"Yep. Easy-peasy." Griz gave him a sideways wink.

"Yeah. I'll just break in, and we'll be great."

"We will." Griz snorted. "It's us. What could go wrong?"

"Don't tempt fate, bear."

"I'm not. I swear." Griz held up one hand in a testify position.

"Good. It shouldn't be a thing, though. Mostly boring shit."

"Yeah. Recording in and out."

"Mm-hmm. Watching the moths around the lights."

"You think?" Griz chuckled. "Did I ever tell you about the bird watching I did for a biology major I knew?"

"No, but you'll have a chance to, mate." And he wanted to know.

"When we get dug in today, I totally will." It didn't take long for them to be off the highway and into an industrial park, where they slid in across from the building they were surveilling.

The place seemed empty all right, but it wasn't dark enough to do anything but settle and watch. They needed to lie low enough to not be seen, but be alert enough to spot comings and goings.

Brock got to work with the cameras, getting them ready to set up.

Griz got the mics and long-range lenses going, as well as laying out a notebook and recorder. They worked well together. It was easy to wait until full dark.

No light. No motion. No one was in that warehouse.

"So now we wait," Griz said. It wasn't a question. He'd never done a stakeout with Griz. It has always been danger and in and out jobs.

"I need to get up there, install cameras, yes?"

"Give it another half an hour, kitty. Don't push it."

"Bossy old bear."

"Safety first." Griz rubbed Brock's leg.

"Safety? What is this safety thing?"

"Mated people think of their mate before doing stupid things." Griz chanted it as if it were a school lesson.

"My mate is a great big grizzly bear. Even if I wasn't super-amazing slinky man, I'd be safe."

"I like your faith in me." Griz stroked his leg again, slow and sensual.

"It's true." Brock knew it in his soul, even if his brain was still in awe.

"It is, but I still want you to try to be careful." Griz chuckled, patting him. "Okay, now you can go do your recon and camera."

"I'm going to shift; it'll be easier. I'll take the bag in my mouth." Brock toed off his shoes, unzipped his hoodie.

"Mmmm, naked time." Griz watched carefully.

"*Sim*, know it." He flexed playfully.

"Oh." Griz's little noise made him have to thump himself.

"Be nice, bear," Brock murmured. "I have to work."

"I'm trying. I want to be very nice."

He stripped out of his pants, showing off some.

Griz growled, the sound raising the hair on the back of his neck.

He shifted, growling right back. *"Bear."*

"Go get 'em... jaguar."

He yowled, grabbed the bag, and then sped across the expanse of the parking lot, using the trees to launch himself onto the roof. He was spry and he knew it, surefooted. A climber.

Griz was not. Not like Kit, who could climb almost anything. Grizzly versus black bear, he guessed.

He crept along the roof to the skylight, and then he shifted back to use his hands. He needed to be able to do fine work with wires. Luckily, he didn't hurt when he shifted.

If he did, this job would suck.

He worked the skylight open, silent as he could be, and he looked down into the warehouse, surprised to find not boxes, but chalk drawings on the floor, candlesticks, skulls. He flowed back to his jaguar form to use his full senses.

What the hell? This wasn't a ring of thieves.

This was.... He sniffed. Incense?

"Griz? Can you hear me?" Deus, he hoped so. This whole situation smelled like a grease fire at a bad diner.

"Right here, lover. What is it?"

"This is wrong." He scanned the camera over the floor.

"What is?" Concern crept into Griz's mental tone.

"Look at the feed on the laptop."

"What the heck is all that?" Griz asked after a little pause.

"Not an up-and-coming business, mate. This is... creepy." He sighed. *"Putting the cameras up."*

"Keep your head down in case someone is there. I'll save stills for Mick."

"On it."

He eased himself onto the catwalk, moving as quickly as he could. Something was very off here, the feeling riding him hard, creeping up the back of his neck.

"I don't like this, Griz."

"Trust your instincts and get out. We'll do what we can remotely."

"Yeah."

A spotlight landed on him, blinding him for a second, and

Brock scrambled back, mentally shouting his alarm. *"They see me! I'm coming back."*

Please let him be coming.

He leaped as hard as he could to another beam along the drop ceiling thingees. The light chased him, and he made a crazed jump for the skylight, his body twisting to reach for the opening.

He grabbed with his claws, which was the only thing that saved him. The screech of them on glass was loud and awful, but he gained the roof.

The SUV was running, and he headed for the comforting sound, the deep rumbling of the engine. They needed to move out. The back of his neck was bristled, his tail a straight line.

"Come on! Now." Griz was growling, deep in his head and out loud.

He leaped into the open door, and Griz yanked it shut before gunning it. God, Griz had long arms.

"Go. Go, Griz. That wasn't a thief." No. No, that was bad hoodoo.

"What the hell, baby? Were they waiting for you?"

"I don't know. How could they be?"

"I don't know." Griz's expression was set and grim in the light from the dash. *"We need to tell Mick."*

"Yes. We need to go home. Make sure no one follows us."

Griz nodded, screaming into a turn, then two and three more. Good man.

Brock focused on his shift, on getting dressed and armed. On getting on the horn with James. "Lost the cameras. Kill them."

"On it. I can keep them active and untraceable."

"Are you sure? I want nothing that can come back to us."

"Of course I'm sure. What the fuck happened?"

"Drawings on the floor, candles. Creepiness. They caught sight of me."

"Shit, man." James was chewing ice, he could hear it. "Okay, if I can't get them cloaked in less than a minute, I'll kill them."

"Good. We're coming in. Get the boss."

"I'm on it." James hung up, and he knew everyone would be in and ready to meet about the situation.

"You okay?" He wanted to feel Griz's arms around him.

"I was worried. Now I want to make sure not to take anything back. I want to stop at a big gas station and sweep the vehicle."

"Okay. I'll go in and grab munchies and a Coke." He was buzzing, his skin too tight.

"Cool. Get me a honey bun and a Fanta orange."

Ugh. "You're a sick bear, honey."

"I am. Feed a fever...."

Brock laughed, heading into the store.

He may have been laughing, but he was watching close, just in case. Better to be separate if there was something in the car, right? *"Be careful."*

"I am, I promise." It looked as if Griz was getting gas, but he was scoping out the car, and Brock knew Griz was looking for both unwanted passengers and devices.

He grabbed Corn Nuts and Fanta, milk and jerky, plus five bags of Doritos in different flavors for the team.

The bored clerk popped her gum at him, ringing up with deliberate lack of speed.

He fought the urge to growl and bare his teeth. No scaring random girls, dammit.

She grabbed the first bag of Doritos, and Brock noticed a tattoo on her hand near her thumb. Where had he seen that symbol? Where had...?

The floor.

The floor on the warehouse they'd just left.

Fuck. Okay. Okay. Fuck.

"Cool ink. What's the design?"

"Some kind of demonic temple thing. My boyfriend drew it for me." She popped her gum again.

"It rocks. Seriously." He needed a picture of it. Brock grabbed his phone, pretending to check a text. The camera made a sound, but the video didn't, and God knew the girl didn't move too fast to catch a visual.

"Thanks." She bagged the last of his stuff. "Have a good night."

"You too. See you." He kept himself lazy and loose, just in case someone was watching, but what he wanted was to run to the car.

Griz was back in the driver's seat, hands on the wheel. Ready.

He slipped in, closed the door, and locked it. "Clear?"

Griz nodded.

"Go. Go, it's not safe."

"Okay." Griz went, managing to gain speed gradually enough not to draw traffic camera attention. "Tell me."

"She had a tattoo—same design that was on the floor in the warehouse."

"She who?"

"The checker in the store."

"Shit. That's a hell of a coincidence." Griz gave him a tight sideways glance. "And I don't believe in those."

"Me either. She said it was some demonic temple thing." Brock hated when he had no idea what was really going on.

"Like Aleister Crowley?" Griz's eyebrows went to his hairline.

"I took video for James."

"Okay. Good. You were fast."

"Well, I had time, as slow as she was checking me out."

Griz chuffed out a laugh, but there was worry pouring off him. That bear had no poker face, at least not with him.

He reached out, hand finding Griz's thigh. "Helluva night, bear."

"I know. So much for our being able to neck while we surveil."

"Right? What the actual fuck?"

They grinned at each other, but Griz still took them the long way, taking almost an extra half an hour to get back to the office.

By the time they pulled into the garage, the entire team was down there, waiting for them.

"What the hell?" Mick bellowed when they stepped out of the SUV.

"You tell me!" Brock met Mick head-on, trusting the wolf to be able to handle his fear. "You said it was a loose-fingered employee! Not some weird-assed cult."

"Cult? Jesus." Mick grabbed him in a bone-creaking hug. "You're both okay?"

"Yeah." He leaned for a second. "It was fucked-up, boss."

"Come on and tell us." Mick weaved his way through the guys. James was already sweeping the car again for devices.

"I brought Doritos for the debrief," Brock said.

"Good deal. We have a jar of queso." Mick sounded wigged-out.

He chuckled, because by the time they got to the big lounge, Kit and Rey were heating up queso dip and setting out salsa. How did they get there so fast?

Griz sat, eyes boring into him as he paced, telling Mick and the rest about the unpleasant surprise he'd found.

"Floodlights." Dylan shook his head. "You think they could see you see you? Or just an impression."

"I hope it was just an impression. I was moving fast."

"Good." Mick still sounded worried.

"It really was super fucked-up, boss. What's the plan?"

"I dunno. Let me call the client. He might simply want to send in the cops."

He nodded. That was a good idea. Fabulous. Something creepy was up. Something they didn't need to be involved in.

"I had to kill the cameras," James said. "I couldn't be sure they weren't follow-backing."

Everyone paused a moment, as if sending up a wee prayer.

"Did you get anything before you shut that down?"

"I'll have to go through the info again." James spread his hands. "I was in a hurry to come see you brothers."

"Okay." He pondered. "Griz did you get anything outside?"

"Couple of vehicle plates to run. I only had time to get a few pictures. I haven't run them yet."

"Get those done, Locke. I don't like the way Brock's hackles are raised." Mick was all grr.

"I brought Doritos, boss." Brock winked, trying to bring the mood lower.

"Well, break them out."

Griz chuckled, pulling out his phone. "Running those plates."

"I'm going to go upstairs and look at that video. I'll holler." James kissed his cheek.

"Okay." He patted that fine butt, and Griz growled a little. *"Stop it."*

"Don't have to. You're mine."

Oh, didn't that feel good? Possessive man. *"I am."*

"I like James, but they all need to know." Griz's fingers were flying.

"I'm not ashamed. Not at all."

"Good." Those warm eyes met his for just a moment, shining with pride.

Goddess, he wanted to curl into bed with Griz, snuggle in

close. They'd spent a few short hours that way, and Brock wanted more.

"Okay, both vehicles belong to a holding company. It's called SNH Conglomerates."

"Do we know the owner?" he asked.

Mick shook his head. "Not yet, but we'll dig."

"Huh. Well, I'll let James know." Brock texted James to let him start looking into the name.

On it. Get some rest, James shot back.

Yeah. "Anything else you want us to do now, boss?" Brock asked.

"Nah. You had your excitement. I'll holler at the client and get back to you. Go on. Be matey."

The fox chuckled softly, Rey winking at him when he mock-glared.

He grabbed Rey up, hugged him. "I brought you Spicy Nacho."

"You're good to me." Rey gave super hugs, had reminded him what it was to be touched. Now he had a bear to touch him, everywhere.

He pecked Rey on the cheek. "I try. Eat up. I'm gonna go snuggle."

"What happened to grumpy kitty?" Dylan teased, plucking Rey away from him.

"I could bite you, if you want," he offered.

"No." Griz's arms wrapped around him. "No biting the wolf. Later, guys."

Then they were moving like one beast up the stairs, Griz's arm around him. He was warming up, his skin too tight, his adrenals reminding him he could have been trapped.

Griz would have come roaring to his rescue, but how big was this thing?

He grabbed Griz's hand as they hit the landing.

"You okay, baby?" Griz asked, squeezing his fingers.

"No. No, that was too close." And it hadn't been all that close. He used to be far more reckless. Like, yesterday.

"Yeah." Griz stopped him, kissing him fiercely for a moment, and he let himself melt into those heavy muscles. This was what he needed: Griz. Here. Now.

They stumbled to his apartment and struggled to get inside. Griz kept tugging at his clothes, which made it hard to walk.

"Please, Griz. Need you." Brock tore at Griz, almost feral.

"I know. I know. I can smell you." Griz lifted him, tossing him toward the bed in a football-style rush. He landed on his hands and feet, yowling.

"Hey, no going all kitty," Griz growled, tearing at his clothes.

"No?" He nuzzled into Griz's shoulder with a purr.

"No, I have plans. Right now."

Oh good. He was ready for plans. Right now. He grabbed Griz and sank dull teeth into his shoulder.

"Oh. More." Griz held him, his voice deep and yearning.

"Mine. My bear." He bit again, harder.

"Yours. So yours." Griz lay back, offering to let him take the lead now, which was sweet and kind of amazing. He allowed himself to melt down over his bear, touching and biting everywhere he could reach.

Griz writhed under him, big body bare in moments under his hands. He nipped all along Griz's collarbone, along the broad rib cage, along one hip. Little marks bloomed along every spot, his marks. He adored that big body, the fuzzy chest, the heavy cock.

He grabbed said cock to stroke it. No biting there. That was too sensitive. Licking, though. Goddess, yes. He could do that right now.

It was so easy to swoop down and lap at the tip of Griz's cock.

Griz moaned, arching up to meet him, making the head slide along his cheek. They stopped short of poking him in the eye, though.

Excellent, he didn't want to have to explain a shiner in the morning.

He wrapped his lips around the head of Griz's dick after he caught it again so he could suck. Hard. Griz tasted rich and male, and the act of suction soothed him, helped him to relax.

"My oral kitty." Griz stroked his hair, voice fond.

"Mmm...." Why argue? It suited them both.

Griz laughed, joyful as hell, then dug in with both heels to lift up. Someone wanted more.

Brock closed his eyes and went down, taking as much as he could.

Those legs spread, the balls under his chin moving. Griz smelled so damn good. All male musk, strong enough to make his nose twitch. "Don't stop now," Griz growled.

"Mmm." Brock hummed. No, he wasn't stopping, unless it was to fuck Griz hard. Now, there was an idea. He could make Griz scream, make his mate roar.

"Please, love. Yes." Griz was urging him on, loving on him.

"Slick?" He hummed softly and began to bob his head.

"Your apartment, baby. Tell me where."

Oh, right. He smiled around Griz's cock, tickled to death. *"Box under the bed."*

"Under!" Griz rumbled and grumbled but moved until one long arm gained the reach Griz needed.

Brock nudged Griz's balls, rolled them and swallowed around his prick.

"Fuck! Brock! Gonna make me come."

That was sort of the point, right?

Griz popped back up to hand him the lube, which was hot as hell, even as he slicked his fingers and began to press them inside.

Eyes wide, Griz watched him, maybe holding his breath.

He worked the slit of Griz's cock with his tongue. *"Okay?"*

"More than okay. Killing me with good stuff."

"Yes. Loving you." He could admit that, here. Now. He pressed in deeper, stroking Griz inside.

"More, baby." Griz spread wide again, really giving him the whole of that body to love on.

"Like this?" He sucked and fingerfucked and gave Griz all he had.

"Yes." Griz said it out loud, voice nothing more than a growl.

Yes. He popped off Griz's cock and surged up, staring into dark eyes. "Now?"

"Now." Griz never looked away, hiding nothing from him, not the need or the love.

Brock pressed inside, grunting as he popped through, the heat almost unbearable. Griz clamped down, pulling him in deep, making his breath whoosh out. Brock yelled, the sound a pure yowl.

"Uh-huh. Fuck me, kitty. Now." Griz grabbed his hips, demanding.

"Pushy bear!" He slammed in, driving Griz hard. He grabbed one leg and pushed it up, giving them even more room. That way he could saw back and forth, giving it everything he had. Griz made the best noises, the sweetest growls.

They were just too hot, burning up together. He was surprised the bed wasn't going up in flames. Griz's hands slipped over his skin, fingers dragging, leaving little bruises in their wake. It felt like being pelted with raindrops.

"Need you," he called. *"Mate."*

"Yes. Oh, baby. Harder. I love you inside me."

The words made him growl and thrust all the harder. All he could do was hold that tight ass, pulling Griz forward, then slapping in. Their skin smacked together, the sounds hot as hell.

"Soon," he rumbled. "Soon, bear."

"Very," Griz agreed, face set in a deep grimace.

Brock found his balance well enough to reach down and begin to stroke Griz's heavy prick, base to tip, over and over. The feel of that big cock in his hand, the way Griz's heartbeat leaped, made him smile.

"Come on. Need you. Now." He made the demand, knowing it would be heard.

"Uhhhnnn!" Griz arched sharply, nearly throwing him off, so he clung to that wide chest, feeling the warm jets of completion splashing on his fingers, between them. Brock drove in a few more times, loving the way Griz's body fluttered around him.

That sensation pulled his orgasm out of him, making him grunt and strain as he pumped himself into Griz.

His stress dissolved, and he melted into his bear's arms.

"That's it." Griz pulled him down, hugging on him. "That's it."

"You have my back, *não*?"

"Baby, I have your everything, but come to work, I definitely have your back." Those big hands cradled him.

"Thank you." He took a deep, deep breath before letting everything go.

"Not a problem at all, baby. Not one." Griz cupped his head, just holding on. Warm. That touch was so warm.

He could nap. Then he was going to figure this thing out.

FIVE

Griz woke up with a headache, which made him realize he'd been neglecting his caffeine habit. Man, he needed a cup of coffee.

Brock had good coffee, and he knew it, all he had to do was get out of bed. *Come on, bear*, he thought. *Ass up. Pee, then coffee.*

He felt around, finding the sheets cool. Brock must be out and about. He hoped he hadn't slept through a meeting. Damn, he was gonna lose this job before he really had it.

Still, it felt damn good, sleeping in his mate's bed.

Griz stretched, clenching and unclenching all his muscles. Right. Bathroom.

He did his business and then luxuriated in a long, hot shower. Griz needed food. Then to find his lover and see what was what.

Berries.

He sniffed.

He smelled berries.

Why did he smell berries?

Griz wrapped a towel around his waist, then headed back out to the main room.

Oh. Oh, coffee and blueberry muffins and his mate. Magic.

"Who made muffins?" he asked, making sure there were plenty before grabbing three.

"Kit. They're good."

"You made me coffee, though. I know it." He moved over to take a kiss. Brock reached up and met him halfway. *Heaven. Muffins, coffee, mate.*

Magic.

The kiss went deep for a second, Brock's tongue sliding in to taste him.

"Mmm. Hey. What did I sleep through?" He'd been hibernating away the adrenaline.

"James is researching. Mick's trying to get a line on the client, and Kit is baking. Dylan and Rey are... not around."

"No. I bet they're alone together like we are." Griz winked before grabbing his coffee.

"That would be a sucker bet, bear."

"I know it." He chuckled, then laughed out loud, feeling awesome.

Brock grabbed another muffin, then fed him half. Oh, so good to him. He munched away, wishing he'd buttered them.

"Does Kit make biscuits?" Butter and honey went on those.

"He cooks almost anything. The fox does too."

"Cool. What do you cook?"

"*Pão de queijo.*" The answer was immediate. "*Feijoada.*"

He blinked. "What are those?"

"Cheese bread and black bean soup." Brock was smiling that humor-the-uneducated smile.

"Oh! I've had the cheese breads in Vegas. At the Brazilian barbecue place."

"Ah. A *rodízio*. Love those. Men with meat on swords."

"Mmm. Meat. And this weird salad with hearts of palm." Griz liked salad bars.

"Yes. I love that shit."

His belly started growling, gnawing on his backbone.

"Muffins not enough, Griz?"

"I can have more." Meat was tantalizing, though. He wanted to watch Brock devour food.

"All you want." Brock's purr suited him to the ground.

"I can cook sausage if we have some. To go with." Griz watched Brock, loving that slinky, heavy-eyed look.

"We might." Brock caught him with this fiery, hungry look.

"Uh.... Might what?" He felt stupid with the need to touch.

"Have sausage." Brock grabbed his cock and squeezed.

"We both do. Have it. That's good, baby." He was all revved up. Again.

"Yeah. How did I stay away from you so long, bear?"

How had they managed? "Simple lack of proximity."

"Immense stubbornness on my part."

He stroked the scars on Brock's back, petting them. Yeah. Brock had been stubborn, but he'd had reason. Total reason. Asshole fox.

"You shouldn't touch."

Griz growled softly. "They're mine to touch, mate." Brock needed to know Griz loved all of him. Even the dumb parts.

The broken parts. The marked parts.

He needed them all.

Brock stroked his hair. "Weirdo."

"Indeed."

"My weirdo, hmm?" Brock nuzzled him, purring low, scenting him.

"So yours." He hugged Brock to him, just... happy. The intense longing for his mate, for his family, was fading.

"You give the best hugs, Griz."

"I am a bear." He laughed, swinging Brock in a wide circle.

"You are." Brock nuzzled in, humming softly.

They were basking like giant lizards, and he loved it. Griz thought Brock did too. The real world would intrude soon enough, he supposed.

"It's waiting for us, you know? Trouble. I think that's why Rey's all stressed out."

"Rey's stressed?" He blinked at the abrupt statement. "Did I miss it?"

"Well, no. I mean, Dylan and Rey are all in their rooms like we are."

"Oh. You just seemed to know something I don't."

"I know Dylan. He's keeping Rey busy. The fox has a sixth sense."

"Like he sees ghosts?"

"No, he has a... like a sense for trouble. Vibrations."

"Like Spidey-sense?" Oh, that would be cool. They could tie him to the top of the car like an alarm and he could just bleat out when anything was coming.

"Yeah, something like that." Brock shrugged. "I guess we need to check in with him at some point."

He gave Brock a curious look, but if his kitty wasn't worried, neither was he. They would wait and have what time together they could before things got busy again.

"I freaked out yesterday. It was ridiculous. Some people dressing up and having rituals. No big."

Uh-huh. He believed that. Not. No, it had to have been super weird in person, and then there was the tattoo at the convenience store.... Yeah. Griz didn't believe in coincidences.

Not even a little.

He wrapped his arms around his mate, the urge to take him to a quiet cave to hibernate huge.

"Caves are in short supply, honey," Brock murmured.

"Mmm. Blankets work. More muffins first." And he really did want that sausage.

"Fair enough, sausage, muffins, blanket fort, and bad TV until they call us in."

"Yes." Griz beamed. This was the life. Thank God he'd taken the chance on that interview with Mick.

————

"Brock. Wake up." Someone was banging on the door, bothering him.

"Shh. Sleeping."

"Brock! Please." He thought it was a fox. Foxes were trouble. Even the good ones.

"Okay. Okay, for fuck's sake." He shoved at the large, hairy thing weighing him down. Bear. Like, really bear.

Wow. Impressive. Also, he was fairly sure all the mattress springs *had* just died.

Thank God Mick had the beavers reinforce all floors and walls and shit and that he was really a jaguar in a human body so he wasn't crushed.

"Shift it, bear."

Griz snorted and grunted but rolled off, leaving him amazed that only one leg and paw had been on him.

The bed groaned and collapsed as he leapt off. He opened the door with a soft growl. "What?"

"Something's wrong with James."

"What?" His mind sharpened, sleep falling away. Brock grabbed a robe, then wrapped it around himself.

"He bit me when I went up to see him."

Like James couldn't nip a little when he was frustrated. "Oh, for fu—"

"No. For real." Rey held out his arm, the bite deep and harsh. *Oh fuck.* Dylan was going to kill James, and Brock was immediately on alert.

"I didn't want Dylan to see until someone else checked in on him." Rey bit his lower lip, clutching his arm to his chest.

"Okay. You go to Kit. I'll talk to James. We'll take care of it." He hoped. *Fuck-a-doodle-doo.*

"Are you sure? I...." Rey looked down. "I have a bad feeling, Brock."

"Yeah. Me too. Go get Kit and then talk to the boss. I'm going to James."

"Sorry." Rey bolted, and he sighed. Poor kid had trauma from the crocs.

"Bear. I need backup."

Griz popped up like the world's biggest, fuzziest jack-in-the-box. He padded across the floor, those big paws sounding like thunder.

He nodded, sinking his fingers into Griz's thick fur for a second, and then he went to find pants.

Pants were important where biting was involved. A robe wasn't gonna cover it. *"Heh. Cover it."*

"Oh, bad, baby. Bad."

"Yeah. Did you hear the fox?"

"James bit him? That's weird, right?" Griz waited by the door.

"More than weird. Rey adores James, and vice versa. They share an office, for fuck's sake."

"Not good...." That big nose was working as if Griz was scenting trouble.

"Yeah. You ready?" Griz could smother any trouble, sort of literally.

"I am. I'll stay like this, just in case."

Yep. Recent experience told him bear trumped big cat. Griz was the only one who could.

Hopefully it would be a nonissue.

He dressed, then headed out, scrubbing his hand over Griz's back on the way. James had to be in his office if he'd been there with only Rey.

It was easy to bound up the stairs to the door and pound on it. "Yo. Brother. Let me in!"

There was no answer, not even a snarl.

"James?" He tried the knob. Locked.

Griz sniffed at the bottom of the door, big head moving from side to side.

"Is it okay? Should I pop it?"

"I don't know. Something is off." Brock wiggled the knob again, but it wasn't going to give. He grabbed his phone and dialed One, and Mick picked up immediately. "I need the key to comms. Now," Brock said.

"You got it." Mick didn't argue, so either Rey had gotten to him or he just trusted Brock. Wow.

He paced for the sixty seconds it took Mick to make his way upstairs, grumbling to Griz and banging on James's door.

"So he bit Rey?" Mick asked.

"Yeah, and he's not answering."

Mick frowned and slid the key card in the lock, the expression deepening as the lights didn't turn green.

"No way." Brock shook the handle. "How could he change it if he was in bitey kitty form?"

"Was he alone? Did Rey say?"

"No. He didn't tell you?"

"No." Mick shrugged. "I sent him to Kit for some first aid."

"So did I. Stubborn fox."

"He is." Mick winked. "Break it down, Locke."

Griz roared for them, standing up tall and huge, and then those giant paws bashed at the door. The door held, but not under the onslaught Griz laid on it after that. Everyone had come upstairs, drawn by the noise, so when the door fell and they found James, they all gasped as one.

James lay on the floor, his fur matted with blood and scored with long, deep slashes. He was breathing, but just barely, his ribs moving up and down shallowly. He was foaming too, his tongue hanging out.

"James!" He roared, and he tried to rush in, but Griz grabbed him.

"Mate! Traps!"

Brock slammed to a halt, the warning ringing in his mind.

"No! Mick, Locke says there are traps."

"What the fuck!" Mick's growl was as frustrated as Brock felt as he jerked to a halt.

"Lock the building up, Dylan!"

"On it!" Rey's big lover raced away. Carrie stood with her hands over her mouth, staring at James.

"Kit, Griz, you start searching. Carrie, get an ambulance. Now." Mick was snarling orders, and Brock put his emotions aside.

Traps.

Search for traps.

Griz sniffed hard, moving into the room one big paw at a time. It was like having the world's biggest pointer when Griz went "boing" and nosed toward something.

There was something set on the floor—a touchpad. He snarled softly and carefully moved, hunting for wires, something.

Mick peered in. "What is it?"

Something hit Brock's nose, and it wrinkled. "Poison. It

smells rancid and dangerous. I need to find it. Get him out of here."

"Okay." Mick came in like gangbusters, scooping up James and hustling out. Moving him was worth it, even if it hurt him.

Brock found the thin glass bottle under James's desk, the damn thing strung up on a lick and a promise.

Griz rumbled, the warning not to touch clear.

"Get out of here, bear. Get everyone downstairs."

"No way. I'm not leaving you."

"Go." He loved the fuzzy son of a bitch. Brock moved gingerly. He knew Rey kept gloves to open the mail sometimes, so he would start there.

He had to get these out of here and then... then what? Where was he going to take this to find out what it was, how it got there?

"Call in hazmat?" That big bear body was vibrating, and he could tell Griz was desperate to get between him and the danger.

"Get your ass out of here, bear." That wasn't a bad idea, really. He wasn't trained to do that sort of shit. Hook it up, yes? Research it? Not so much.

"Come on. We'll seal it off and call someone in."

"Smart."

He could feel Griz's stress levels drop as he agreed. Really, though, experts would be so much better equipped to deal with this shit, and he wanted to check on James.

He didn't understand what had happened here, how someone had snuck in. That? That was his job. To find out what the fuck was going on with the building.

Brock's eyes narrowed. There was too much in and out already to print the door and the stairs....

"No. The air vents."

"What?"

"I need to go back in, Griz. It got in through the air vents."

"No. No, you can do something remotely or call in...."

"I have to know if they're there. I have to find out." He stroked Griz's ear. "I'm going to shift and go up."

"No. It stinks, Brock. You need gloves. A mask."

"What if he's still in the place? Whoever he is."

Griz stared at him, those black button eyes so worried. *"I'll shift and suit up to be your backup on the ground."*

"Thank you. If he's here, he'll run."

Griz nodded that big head, then backed carefully out of the room. He would have to have clothes and a mask, at the least.

Then Brock went back into James's office and stripped down, pulled a chair over, and looked for the hint of where the asshole had slipped in.

"You're supposed to be waiting."

"Huh?"

He was sort of waiting. In a way.

"I'll be right there." He thought Griz's mental voice was maybe a tiny bit exasperated.

"You're working the exits. Pay attention." Oh, there. He saw one of the ceiling tiles was cracked.

"No, I'm supposed to be right under you while someone else does the exits."

He knew what Griz meant, but he had to concentrate now, so he tuned out his lover.

Brock climbed up, shifting as he jumped, his nose wrinkling immediately as his eyes tried to adjust to the darkness. The smell up here was actually less intense, but there was another odor. A musky scent.

He stilled, preparing himself to hunt. There were symbols sketched all through the air ducts.

"He's here."

"Be careful!"

What else could Griz say? They were both used to bad situations and wet work. Being in love didn't change that.

"Duct metal has sigils." The scent trails led everywhere.

"Get out of there. If this is a magick user, you are so not qualified to stop it."

"I don't know if I can get out." He was fairly sure it knew he was here. The smell of stress was enough to make him gag.

"Stop, then. Wait where you are."

Brock froze. Yeah. Griz had a point. If the guy was trying to get away.... But what if they weren't and were trying to get to the rest of the team. Did he chance it?

He crept forward, nose and whiskers twitching.

The musk intensified, almost like a male cat had sprayed.

His lips curled, and his cat took over, insisting that someone was intruding on his territory. He wasn't feeling any effects of any fumes or sigils, so he kept moving. The faster he moved, the stronger the smell of panic grew.

A light as bright as the surface of the damn sun flared in front of his face, almost knocking him over. As a stopping tactic, it worked great.

He snarled, squeezed his eyes closed, and crouched, getting ready to spring.

There was a scurry of sound, and a blast of air ruffled his whiskers. Was it blowing poison at him? Brock scrambled back just a few feet, trying to decide what to do.

"Brock! Mate!"

He scrabbled on the metal duct, the damn thing groaning under his weight.

Brock had no idea where he was in the building now, though he couldn't have gotten far.... Two long, lithe forms slid past him, another blinding flash of light making him paw at his face.

"Griz!" The world was shuddering all around him.

"I'm coming!"

With no idea what that meant, Brock dug in with his claws, but the metal buckled beneath him, a sharp crack sounding.

Good thing he always landed on his feet.

Actually, when the ceiling broke under him and he crashed through, this time he landed in Griz's arms.

"Well, hello."

SIX

Griz ran like he usually only did when his own hide was on the line. He knew where Brock was from the noise above, and he slid into place just in time to catch his lover when he fell. Good thing his bear strength could be called upon even in his human form.

That was two fifty of cat.

Those bright green eyes blinked at him. *"Mate."*

"Hello, lover. Are you okay?" Brock seemed fine, if confused.

"They're up here."

"They?" That explained a lot.

"Yes. I smelled two. I think they're on their way out of the ducting and the building."

"Mick is going to lose it." This place was supposed to be impenetrable.

Speaking of Mick and losing it, their fearless leader appeared. "What the hell is going on here!" Mick barked.

"I have no idea, boss." Griz put Brock down, nice and easy. "Something in the vents, Brock says. He says there's two."

And there was poison. Griz wanted to start tearing at the vents, but that would destroy shit.

"The EMTs have James on some kind of drip. The bomb squad is coming to deal with his desk. They want us all out of the building. They want to take James to the hospital, but I don't trust them to keep him safe." Mick's face was hard as stone.

"I want them out. Now." Brock's eyes glittered at him.

"I bet they are." Griz had a feeling they were long gone, in fact. "Come on, mate. We all need to talk."

"Downstairs. Outside. Brock, clothes, man." Mick was all wolf—growling and pacing and barking orders.

Brock sniffed, then turned, tail stiff, and headed out the door.

"Meet you downstairs, mate."

"Okay." He glanced at Mick. "You coming too?"

"Yes. Come on. What the fuck, man? I mean, seriously. What the fuck?"

"I don't know." Griz was getting a little paranoid about what they'd gotten into on their truncated job. "What does the fox say?"

"Dylan says Rey dreamed about someone watching them."

"Shit." That meant someone had been in the whole building, observing.

He hated leaving Brock somewhere alone in the building, he hated this whole poison thing, and he hated being watched.

"Come on, man." Mick tugged at his arm. "It sucks, but we've got to rendezvous with the rest of the team."

"I know." *"Hurry, mate. I want you close."*

"I'm coming." Brock's mental voice was distracted.

"Mate?"

"I'm coming."

"Now!" Griz broke away from Mick, turning back into the building.

"Locke? Locke, what the fuck?"

"I need to find Brock." If Brock was following that kitty curiosity.... God, that was a whole saying, and it never ended well.

"He's on his way, right? God damn it. I'm going to skin him alive."

Yeah, no. No one was skinning his lover, but Griz might spank him. Hard. Later.

His kitty was hunting; Griz could tell. There was a constant hum of curiosity, interest. This was bad, though, because whoever he was hunting had already set traps. Damn it.

"Brock! Get your ass out!"

"Griz?"

There was his cat.

"Now, damn it!" He roared the words, finding his inner black ops leader, who'd been quieted by the mate bond.

Brock snarled back, but he could feel his mate, growing closer and closer.

That was all he wanted. He would pick Brock right up and carry his ass out of the building. This was... there was a prickling on the back of his neck.

"Mate...."

"Something's wrong. Mick. Mick, something's wrong." The little fox snapped out the words, and the big wolf moved immediately.

"In the vehicles. Everyone on their toes!"

Griz growled. "Not without Brock." He wasn't leaving.

"No. Not without Brock, but I'm going to make sure we're defensible."

"I'm a bear." He was pretty defensible on his own. "Go.

I'll catch up." They were wasting time. *"The fox says something is wrong. Where are you?"*

"Coming! I'm driving them down!"

God damn it! Why was Brock so fucking stubborn? Mick was yanking at him, and Kit was lumbering toward them, clearly ready to help.

"Out the side vent, second floor, west wall."

"Dylan, Kit, with me." Griz raced around to the west of the building, his mind settling into combat mode.

About the time he got set, two of the biggest weasels he'd ever seen wiggled out of the vent. Okay. Weasels. He needed a fox. "Rey! Help!"

Rey came zipping around the corner, and to his utter glee, managed to leap, shifting in midair to catch one at the back of the neck and start shaking.

"Don't kill it. We need it!" He went after the other, who was darting at Rey, biting and clawing.

Dylan barked at Rey, taking the weasel in hand. "Stop it or we'll let Rey have you."

"Bomb squad's here. Yay." Carrie sounded so thrilled.

"Cool. We have two of the unsubs. I want my mate out of the building." Griz started back to the building. *"Bomb squad. Come on!"*

"Uh...."

"What? No uh. Get out." Griz had taken all he could. *"I'm coming to get you."*

"Good idea. I'm stuck. Like seriously."

"Aw shit. Civilian in the building!" Griz roared. "Wait until we get him out!" He pelted back around to the main entrance. *"Where are you?"*

"In the vent outside Mick's office."

He would tear out the ceiling panel with his bare hands. Then the vent if he had to.

"There are tons of sigils up here. Tons."

"Baby, I don't like this." Griz rounded the corner outside Mick's office. "Bang for me!"

Clang. Clang. And then a roar. Oh, very nice.

He leaped, swatting at the ceiling tiles. He knew they dropped the ceiling to hide wires and such, but he needed to talk to Mick about that industrial, exposed look.

Oh. Tail. Pissed-off tail. It lashed back and forth, and he hopped up and grabbed the end, tugging lightly.

"Mate! Stuck! Out!"

"I've got you." He thought he did, anyway.

"Here, lift me up. Dylan has the weasels." Rey smiled at him when Griz jumped.

"What?" He didn't follow.

"I can undo the clamp on the vent rather than just tearing it out." Rey winked. "Mick will get grumpy."

"Oh." Griz looked up, pointed. "He's a little grumpy right now."

"Hoist me." Rey reached for his shoulders, and he cupped his hands to let Rey have a leg up. "Hey, Brock, it's me. I'm going to help."

That tail flicked as if in understanding, and it only took Rey maybe ten seconds to unclamp two sections of the venting. "Look out below!" Rey called.

Griz braced himself to catch, and his kit kept his claws in, so that worked. Rey skittered down and out of the way.

Shit, they ought to join the circus.

Maybe he had and he just didn't know it. The impression was reinforced when two things happened simultaneously. Brock licked his nose, and Mick shouted, "I like you, Locke, but if you're gonna spend all your time holding grumpy kitty, we're gonna have a problem. Get your asses out of the building."

Brock snarled, rolling out of his arms and chewing Mick out in pissed-off kitty.

"Out." Mick pointed, and they all trooped out of the building.

"What a mess...," Griz murmured.

"Hey! I caught them, didn't I? Drove him out."

"You did good. Am I going to get fired?" He hadn't even completed one case.

"Stop it, Locke. You're one of mine."

"Thanks, Mick." He meant it. "What now?"

"We let the bomb squad do their job. We keep James as comfortable as we can." Mick grimaced, turning away.

"We eat the weasels? I'd share with the fox."

"No, we do not eat them. We question them." Brock needed to get unfuzzy.

"My idea's more fun...."

"Brock...." He fought a grin.

"Nom nom nom."

"Brock, will you please go to the van and get dressed." Mick was going to throttle someone.

"You want to come... pet me?" Someone had scared himself and now he was being a shit. Adrenaline was a funny thing, and what Griz knew that no one else did, was that it was the being trapped that had scared Brock so much.

"I will never leave you behind, mate," he swore, and Brock shivered, disappearing into the van.

Griz followed. Fucking fox. Not Rey. Griz liked him. Brock's ex, on the other hand....

That evil motherfucker deserved to die for all the terrible scars he'd left on Brock, inside and out. Griz would do the job too, if he ever saw the jerk.

"He'll be right out," he told Mick.

"Good. I want this shit buttoned down."

"I know." He could get to the weasels, but since he was being allowed, he kept an eye on the van, wanting to be close to Brock. His mate was like a beacon, a throbbing light.

He wanted them together. They needed each other so badly, now they were letting the bond form again.

This time they weren't going to be torn apart. They were a unit, mated at a cellular level. He would make sure Brock never had any more second thoughts.

"Locke! Pay attention, goddamn it!"

"What!" Griz turned to Mick. "What? Sorry."

"What did Brock find up there? Besides weasels."

"Lots of sigils. Someone's spelled the whole place." He worried about that. "I think we should all hole up in a safe house until we know what's what."

"Again? No. No, this is our place, dammit. How could they get in after all the work we did? Who the hell sent them?"

"So what do we do, boss?" That was Kit, coming to stare at the building.

"We figure out what the fuck this is all about." Brock came out of the van, spitting and snarling. "How's James?"

"Sick. His body's trying to fight this poison, but so far we can't identify it." Mick shook his head, looking grim.

"Can they give him a transfusion? Like they do for chemo patients? I'll do it for him." Brock offered immediately, and Griz wanted to just snarl.

"I don't know." Mick spread his hands.

Kit shook his head. "They won't try that yet, but it may come to that. Right now I'd be afraid his body would fight the new blood like it is the poison."

"So, let's go find out how to neutralize it." Brock smiled, the look icy cold and vicious.

"You got it." Mick headed back to where Dylan had caged the weasels.

The fox was stalking them, vocalizing constantly, threatening them, and Dylan was watching, arms crossed. Who knew little Rey could be so fierce?

"All right, you guys can shift and tell us who you're

working for and what they want, or we can figure out what combination of drugs and shock therapy make you shift...." Mick was also damn fierce.

"Hot, isn't it?" Brock raised one eyebrow. "I think we could feed Rey bits until someone screams." Lord, his mate was wonderfully evil.

The one weasel scratched at the cage, pacing in front of the other, and as soon as it moved, Rey pounced. He bounced up straight-legged, then gnawed at the weasel cowering in back.

So did they take it alone, since it was clearly the coward, or would the other be better since it was protecting its partner in crime?

"Boss?" Kit's voice was quiet, gentle. "Can they shift in the little cage?"

"No. We have to take one out." Mick's voice was a growl.

"Then let's do it. I want James back to normal." Brock's teeth were growing, shining.

Griz nodded. "Okay, someone grab the one at the back and hold him against the bars."

Kit stared. "No biting. If you bite, I will be very unhappy."

The weasel snapped its teeth.

"I got that one," Dylan murmured, his expression amused. He grabbed the stationary weasel. "Guard the front, Rey."

Rey bounced, the sharp little teeth flashing. He settled in front of the cage opening, so Kit popped it and caught the weasel when he would have bolted. "Close it, Locke!"

Griz sprang forward to close the cage.

Brock leapt over the cage and stared, baring his teeth. "You have ten seconds. One."

The weasel wiggled, the air shimmering around it. It began to morph in Kit's hands, growing larger.

They all circled him, except Rey, who was on the other weasel like white on rice.

Griz blinked when they could finally see a human. Who was a woman, not a man.

Brock didn't seem to care. He started growling, teeth bared and surprisingly sharp, for a human form. Had Brock gotten poisoned too? James had started biting....

"Mate? Mate, relax."

"They hurt James!"

"I know, but Mick might think you've gone rabid."

"Let me go!" the woman spat, even as Kit wrapped his big shirt around her.

"What did you do?" Brock got into her space, and she pushed back into Dylan.

"What we were hired to do. Please, don't hurt him. He's my twin. I need him."

"Details, lady." Mick barked. "Now!"

She hissed through her front teeth. "I don't know shit."

"I don't buy it," Mick said. "You made magick sigils and you poisoned a team member. That's specific. Tell me."

Brock's deep *grrrr* noise split the air, the warning perfectly clear.

She shivered, her thin body shaking. "His name is Hetrick. He owns a warehouse full of magick shit."

The wild fury that filled Brock's mind was the only warning Griz got before Brock pounced.

"Mate!" Griz jumped, keeping Brock from tearing anyone apart.

"Get him out of here," Mick snapped. "Now, Locke."

Griz lifted Brock off his feet, yanking him back toward the van. "Brock. Baby. You need to calm down."

"Motherfucker. I'm going to rip out his spleen."

"No, you're going to explain to me what's going on." He didn't like how Brock was damn near foaming.

Brock tore at his hair. "The client."

"Right. The guy with the warehouse."

Brock began to growl again, the lean body so tense. "And the cheating wife. Why is he after us?"

"Hey. Hey, we have to think, baby. I need you to breathe." That was so not fair, and he knew it, but he was flying blind. He needed intel.

"Think. I want to know where he is, and if she doesn't tell me, I'll rip her throat out. He hurt James. Why? What the hell is he doing?"

"I know, but that does us no good." He put iron in his voice, like he would back in the bad old days of wet work.

Brock growled softly, and Griz could feel the hurt, the worry for his friend.

"He's coming after us. Why?" Griz started working through things in his head. "And what do we have to do with whatever he's up to?"

Brock stilled, head tilting. "I don't know. I... the wife. That's where we start, after we make that weasel bitch tell us what the poison was."

"Okay. Okay, we start there." Griz liked the plan. Action but not running off in all directions.

"James is like a brother to me." The single quiet sentence made him want to roar.

Griz tugged Brock to him. "We won't let him die."

"I believe you. I believe in you, bear."

"I know." He took the kiss he desperately needed before they had to get down to business.

Brock's eyes flew open, the expression fierce and open, wild. He felt everything so damn deep.

"Yes. Right here, mate. Your mate."

"Yes." So clear. So strong. "Mate."

They needed to go interrogate the weasels. They could do this together. They could do anything together.

Then they would find that evil son of a bitch, and Griz would make him pay for hurting his new family. In fact, he was looking forward to getting his hands on the rotten wolf and finding out why he was after them.

"What the fuck is going on with you two? Seriously. Have you lost your minds?" Mick's eyes were alight with fury.

Brock nodded slightly. "Yeah. I'm just—you know how I feel about James. He could die."

For a single, wild second, Griz could see Mick's wolf, and he got it, completely, why Brock had given this man his loyalty.

Mick's expression went stony again. "Okay. Kit, I want you on James. Dylan, I want you on Hetrick. Call in contractors if you have to, because I know you want to stay close to Rey. I want to know everything about that bastard. Everything, not just what's in our dossier. Fox, stay on the weasels. I know you want at them, Brock, but Dylan and Rey have a way, and we have to turn them in to the authorities soon. I want you and Griz on finding out what happened with our building. We will not lose another fucking place this soon. We're all moving to a safe house to sleep."

Griz nodded. "As soon as the cops are done. Right now we're heading to that warehouse, eh, kit?"

Brock nodded back, mouth a grim, straight line. "We are. If you think Dylan and Rey have a line on the weasel thing."

"They'll do this. We're going to bust in and cause chaos."

"Yep. We're going to tear the place down with our bare hands." Finally, blessedly, Brock smiled.

Griz chuckled. "Let's get Oscar Mike."

"Yeah. I want some fucking answers."

They headed out, the day a complete clusterfuck, but his mate was safe. For now. That was the most important thing.

Christ, he needed to figure this shit out.

SEVEN

The world was a dark and dangerous place, and Brock knew it, but today not even the promise of his mate could make things better.

This whole mess gave him the willies. The tactics reminded him of his ex.

Brock had been wet behind the ears and horny as hell when Malvino Oliveria had sunk claws into him and ripped him in two. Now he was older, and he had fucking rage. This bastard Hetrick was coming after them?

Brock would show him what was what. He would happily tear the motherfucker in pieces and leave him to bleed out.

Brock wasn't about to go backward after they'd rebuilt the whole business from the ground up. He had a pack, Mick's misfit pack, and he had Griz. He would wage war like no one had ever seen.

Griz glanced at him sideways. "Where do we arm ourselves?"

"In my rooms." He slipped in the side door and jogged up the stairs before Griz could complain about the cops.

Griz followed without a word. His lover was focused in

work mode, he had to admit. They made their way up, silent and quick. He opened his rooms and went to the gun safe hidden behind a bookcase. He wasn't going in blind this time.

"What about magicks like in the air ducts?" Griz murmured. "What do we have for that?"

"Nothing. Who the fuck does this?"

"This guy, apparently. Better than dire crocs." Griz said it deadpan, but by the time he glared over, Griz was grinning.

"*Deus*, you're so funny. *Engraçado*."

"I am." Griz nodded firmly, checking the grip of a Glock.

Brock loaded his ankle holster and his shoulder holster, and then he slipped a couple of knives on his belt.

"Let's stop by the kitchen," Griz said, surprising him.

"Not the time for the munchie, *doce*."

Griz rolled his eyes, then turned on his heel and headed off. Brock followed, nose and eyes working. Griz wasn't mad, at least not at him, and he thought his lover wasn't hungry either.

It said something that he trusted Griz enough to pad along behind.

They got to the kitchen, where Griz began rummaging. "Salt. Sage. Basil is good for exorcism...." Griz loaded spices into a bag.

"Are you serious?" Huh. Maybe Locke was onto something. Did they have any real silverware?

"Yep. Oh, lemons. If the magical cleansing doesn't work, I can squirt them in someone's eyes."

"I like it. Grab some limes too." Who knew when they'd come in handy?

Griz took a whole ton of stuff, including minced garlic. They would have to shop for Kit and Rey, who cooked, before they came back.

"We'll get some holy water on the way."

"Is it still holy after you touch it, bear?" he teased.

"Shut up." Griz bared those straight, white teeth. Made him think things. Bad things to be thinking when he was hunting bad wolf.

"I just want to make sure you won't burst into flames in the church...."

"What church?" Griz raised his brows.

"Uh... the holy water's in St. Francis, right?"

"Oh, right." Griz snorted. "I was all confused for a moment." And disappointed, if he was reading Griz right. Weird. Maybe Griz had caught his naughty thoughts and wanted to get busy.

He moved closer, rumbling in his chest. *"Mate?"*

"Nothing. Nothing, I swear." Griz bent to kiss his ear. *"Come on."*

He purred softly, head bumping his lover's arm.

Griz relaxed, and they were on their way out to the van. Boom.

He told himself there was no reason to believe this Hetrick guy was anything but lucky. They'd been on guard, so how could he have gotten to them so easily?

"Stop it. I have your back."

"I'm fine." Brock just wanted to bite something.

Griz pulled in at the church and grabbed a water bottle. "Be right back. Don't think too much."

"Be careful." He couldn't lose Griz. Not now.

"I will, baby." Griz jogged off, his combat boots clacking on the asphalt.

He didn't know what the hell he was going to do. He didn't even know how to begin. Brock checked the rearview, then looked at where Griz had disappeared. First they had to clear the warehouse, maybe figure out what kind of magick Hetrick was using.

Maybe they'd burn the goddamn thing down.

Now, there was an idea. No magical bullshit required.

A match, a can of gasoline, and a little luck. Fire was a great cleanser, right?

"What are you grinning about?" Griz asked, climbing back into the vehicle.

"Molotov cocktails. You know how long it has been since I blew something up?"

"Brock...." Griz's tone held warning, but Brock heard laughter in his mind.

"Hmm? You remember how fun that is, right? Kaboom?"

"I do, actually. We might need evidence this time." So much logic.

"Let me have my little fantasy."

"Sure." Griz got their wheels rolling again. "Plan?"

"We break in, take pictures, shut it down." It was a good plan. He liked it.

"Mmm. Okay." Griz liked to pretend he was meticulous, but he liked to play cowboy too.

"We could create a *teeny* explosion...."

Griz hooted. "As a diversion. Fine."

"You're so good to me." He ran one hand up along Griz's thigh, feeling better already.

"I try. I like to keep the pump primed, you know?" Griz took his hand, steering easily with the other hand.

"Is that a euphemism, bear?" He was cracking himself up.

"It is. Was it good?" Griz winked broadly.

"*Perfeito*." He was all over that shit.

"Go me!"

The closer they got to the warehouse, the tenser Brock became. What if that miserable son of a bitch was waiting for them and tried to hurt his mate?

"Easy, mate. Easy. We'll make it work."

"I know. He knows this is getting to me too, I assure you." Brock tapped his fingers on the dash. "What is he getting out of it?"

"I have no idea. Kit is looking into that part."

"I know. Sometimes it's so weird to have a pack. I still think I'm solo."

"Well, here I am to save your ass." Griz kind of sang the words, and Brock thought maybe they were a cartoon thing, but he couldn't remember what.

"And why am I here?" he teased.

"To blow shit up and love me." Griz was so not teasing, he thought.

"I do, you know. I have for a long time."

"I know." Griz reached over to squeeze his thigh. "Which is why you'll be careful."

"Go in. Gather information. Right?"

"Yes, and be ready to blow shit up and toss holy water if we need a diversion." Griz grinned broadly at him.

"I'm all in." And worried.

"Okay. We'll park close but out of sight." Griz gunned it, getting them really rolling out on the highway.

"They'll have fewer places to hide in the daytime."

"Right. I wonder how far the net spreads? I mean, the gas station was a shocker." Griz's mouth set in a grim line.

"Do you think he runs a cult?" Why would an import/export guy with a cheating wife run a cult? It made no sense. None at all.

"No, I think someone like him is using magick users or a cult to do his dirty work." They pulled off the highway, Griz's shoulders tighter the closer they got.

"Yeah. That makes more sense."

"I think so from what you've said. This way he could come after us, and it would look like an accident. You figured out the thing too fast at the warehouse, though, and they had to try the office."

"And James. Dammit." It burned his ass that his brother-at-heart was hurt. Again.

"I'm sorry, baby." Griz parked, and Brock looked around, orienting himself.

Yeah, so was he. This wasn't a job gone bad. This was hell on earth, and he was feeling like it was his fault for maybe pissing this Hetrick guy off.

"Nope. No blaming." Griz took his hand. "Focus. We have to do this professionally."

"I wasn't thinking at you, butthead."

"No, I know, but I could feel it." Griz shrugged. "Mate-bond hazard."

"Yeah. Fucking weird." And wonderful. He guessed that was how he could feel that weird sadness in Locke sometimes. He still needed to ask about that.

"I like it." Griz began arming himself with magick repellents.

Brock relied much more heavily on the whole practical thing. Firearms, blades, and his wits. He checked his Glock, hearing his old team leader in his head. "If you have to check it right before a firefight, you aren't taking good care of it."

Griz chuckled. "Ah, the words of the infamous arms master Zane. Man, he's still a ballbuster."

"Yeah. I miss him sometimes." The trust between them had been shattered, though, and wasn't fixable.

"I did my last out-of-town job with him." Griz shook his head. "Something is broken."

"Lots of things are broken, mate, including me."

"Grumpy kitty." Griz climbed out of the SUV, holstering the side arm he'd laid on the console. "Come on."

"Right. Time to exorcise some assholes." No one hurt his people. No one.

Griz nodded, motioning for him to lead the way. His bear had his back. They slid through the overgrown lot between the parking lot and the warehouse, staying low. They wouldn't be able to avoid cameras, but he'd had the impression if there were any, they were inside.

Besides, if these fucks were magical, they'd know, right?

Right.

Griz growled low, stopping him in his tracks for a moment.

"Mate?" He looked everywhere, eyes darting madly.

"On top of the building opposite the warehouse—there's a lookout."

He found the glint of light, then growled deep in his chest. *"You want me to take him out?"*

"Yeah. I'll get us in the door." He could feel Griz's trust, deep inside him.

Brock sank into the grass, moving like a snake, quick and silent. When he had a shot, he took it, the glint of light disappearing in a second.

There would be no blitz attack unless it came from him and Griz.

"Target down." He intended to finish this. Now.

"The doors are unlocked. Someone is waiting for us."

"Then it's time to go say hello. You be careful, bear."

Bear indeed. He could feel the rush of it when Griz shifted, when the man became the bear. Someone was going in hot.

Brock hit the back door at the same time as Griz crashed through the front. He went in human this time, because he needed the weapons. What the heck had Griz done with his piece?

"Hidden outside. Be good."

"I'm always good, butthead."

"True." He could feel Griz's nose move, that sense of smell so strong.

The warehouse appeared empty, but Brock knew better. His whole self screamed that they weren't alone. What the fuck was the endgame here? His gut told him this guy seemed to be playing to maim, not kill.

Brock moved along the wall, staying in the shadows as he waited for the trap to spring.

A flash-bang grenade went off, damn near blinding him for a long moment. Shit, if he'd been in cat form, he'd be almost crippled by it. As it was, he had to crouch down and run for cover. He kept his weapon ready, but he was running blind, and he didn't have time to hunt his bond with Griz. He had to trust his lover to do his job.

They'd done it before; they'd do it again.

He kept his eyes closed, trying to focus, hear something.

There was a roar, and when he opened his eyes, he could make out the heavy grizzly form of his Locke, staggering under the weight of a hunting net.

Oh, he didn't fucking think so. He grabbed his piece and picked off one of the bastards trying to hurt his mate. The guy cried out and went down, but *Jesus*, they were swarming like ants, these people.

"*Fight them,* amante. *Fight them.*" He'd be damned if he let them win.

He heard Griz roar again, the sound bouncing crazily around the big, open room. That was an intimidating sound. Good man. Bear.

Three more shots sounded, three more assholes went down. He could do this. They would clean out this nest of fucking vipers and find out what the fuck was going on.

Griz lashed out, huge claws catching on the netting, tangling him up even more. Brock growled, wanting to shift, but he would free his mate better as a man, and he knew it.

He moved through the shadows, laying down what he hoped was a maddening spray of bullets, aimed to distract the bad guys, but not hurt his bear.

He needed that net off. They had to fight together.

The cultists were like cockroaches, scrambling around madly. At least the evil fuckers were focused on Griz, leaving him to help.

He'd cut down another two, ready to swoop in and free Griz, when a blow caught him and sent him winding. Brock staggered, but didn't go down. He jumped sideways, trying to see who'd hit him, but between the hit and the flash-bang, he couldn't focus worth a damn.

Another blow disoriented him, and he knew it had to be a shifter. Something fast. The rest of these guys were slow. Maybe drugged or something, but this one was damn quick.

He struck out behind him, catching something with the butt end of his gun. The thud and sound of pain was delicious.

Brock whirled, ready to run to Griz. *"Mate!"*

"Here. Hurry!"

He followed the thought, scrambling toward his lover.

Something whizzed past his ear, but it wasn't a bullet, so he ignored it. He finally made it to Griz's side and tore at the net.

"There's too many. We have to get out."

Somehow.

"Get the net where I can slash it. I'm too tangled." Griz's frustration was palpable.

He whipped out his knife, trying to cut the net away and free up Griz's arms. He was dizzy, though, and taking blows with every second he wasn't on the offensive.

Griz grunted, slashing at the net, which finally fell to shreds. Thank God.

"Now. Now, mate." Griz started barreling for the door.

He almost hopped on and rode, but he pushed one hand into Griz's ruff instead, staggering into a run. He was losing blood from somewhere. Fast.

"No bleeding. Hurry. We're getting you home."

We don't have a home. The thought was sudden and immediately discarded. Bullshit. He had more than a home. He had a pride. They would help him and Griz. Heal him so they could hit these assholes again.

"Yes, mate." The thought gave him a burst of strength, enough to stay with Griz.

Griz took him right to the SUV, a huge, shaggy beast, then shrank, catching him when he slumped. "In. In, Brock. Now."

"In." Brock blinked up, a spattering of Portuguese pouring from him as he landed in the cool confines of the vehicle.

Griz slid naked behind the wheel, grabbing the keys from him when he held them over the back seat. "We're going home. I've called in reinforcements."

"Reinforsh—" He couldn't make his tongue work.

"Don't you fade on me, soldier!"

"Não." He would stay. He wasn't leaving again. He belonged here, and Griz wanted him.

"Always wanted you."

"I... know." His breath came hard. He'd waited too long.

His cat took him in a rush, and he slumped to the seat, tail flopping down onto the floorboards.

"I got you, lover. Hang in there."

He *rowl*ed softly. By his toenails.

Griz chuckled at him, and he wondered what his lover had meant by reinforcements.

Brock supposed he'd just suck it up and wait to find out.

————

Griz felt pretty damn weird driving naked. He was a big shaggy bear, so he was a big shaggy guy too. *Please God, don't let me get pulled over.*

Mick and the others were waiting for him at a bug-out

building downtown, where there should be enough traffic to let them gather unnoticed and get Brock some help.

God, how had this all gone tits up?

He didn't really even have to ask that. They'd gone in pissed off and loaded for bear—pun intended. They needed to be more strategic. Careful. Methodical. That was assuming Brock didn't bleed out before they got to the safe house.

He forced himself to focus on the road, on traffic. He was no use to Brock if he wrecked. His mind raced as he drove, running scenarios on who this mystery client was, who was doing this.

When he was going to rip the head off the bastard who was hurting his pack.

The pain deep in his soul had just started to fade. He'd always wanted a family.

And now they were one. Man, that was a cool thing, that Mick's pack accepted him.

He sure hoped so, anyway.

Griz slid into the lot at the safe house like a runner sliding into third base. He needed help, and he needed it now.

Mick charged out to meet them, his face set in deep lines of concern. "Jesus. Let's get you two inside."

"He's hurt. Please." He grabbed Brock and hauled him up.

"Come on. Kit's a pretty good medic." They stormed inside, a weird little parade of muscle, Kit peeling off, presumably to get supplies.

"He is. Friend! I need help!" He went right for the other bear. "Where do you want him?"

"In the bedroom here. On the bed so I can give him an exam."

"How's James?" Brock would want to know.

"Resting quietly. He'll be okay. His body is healing."

"You got the type of poison?"

"It seems most likely distillation of plants. Rhododendron and chrysanthemum." Mick shook his head. "Old school and pretty damn effective on kitties."

"But reparable?" *Repairable? Fixable?*

"Reversible, yeah." Mick stared down at Brock, face grim. "He'll be all right."

"He will." He had to be; Brock was his mate.

Kit tore into the room, first aid kit in hand. "Shot?"

"I'm not sure. I just ran home. Here. To you."

"Good." Kit grinned at him. "Help me get what's left of his clothes off."

"On it." He stripped Brock down, murmuring softly whenever his kit growled. He stroked that heavy pelt, looking with his fingers for a wound.

There were dozens of bumps and lumps—his cat had taken one hell of a beating—but nothing that he'd—*whoa*.

"Dart."

"Shit. Gimme." Kit took the tiny feathered thing from him, then sniffed it. "Okay. Okay, I think this is the same thing that got James."

"Fix him." Before Brock started biting, preferably.

"I will. I'm going to give him a mild sedative. He weighs more than James, so it shouldn't take him too deep. Then I can synthesize his antidote and make sure it's the right dose." Kit was calm, but Griz heard his heart pounding.

"Good. Good. Do what you need to. You're okay, man. You got this." Trust was important. Faith. Love.

Those dark eyes flashed to his, and Kit smiled. "I do. Thanks, man."

"You got it, brother."

Kit took a little of Brock's blood, then gave him a shot. That tail stopped lashing minutes later, Brock relaxing.

"I'll stay with him. Mick needs to talk to you."

"Mick can get his happy ass in here, then." He wasn't leaving Brock.

"Mick is still right here, assholes."

They both jumped. They'd been so caught up they hadn't realized Mick had stayed.

"Oh, excellent. Boss, who the ever-loving fuck are these people?"

"Pull up a chair."

Kit left them, so Griz headed for a pair of chairs in the corner of the room, needing a sit-down with Mick.

"I don't know for sure why, but I know it's Hetrick. Our erstwhile client."

"The wolf with the cheating wife?" How on earth did that shit track?

"Yeah. I don't know a motive, but the timeline is matching up, and the weasels are sure that's who hired them."

"So we're sure he's the asshole behind this, yes?"

"Behind the warehouse and the poison, yes." Mick shrugged. "I mean, I can't imagine who would hate us this much, aside from the tiger, Patel. The one you helped us catch, but he's in jail."

"Us or the kitties, who seem to have taken the brunt?" It was a fine distinction.

"Either. Or both. I mean, this wolf client was damn mad. Maybe he has a grudge we don't know about." Mick looked like he felt. Angry that they didn't have immediate answers.

"Then we need to go get him, boss. And find out."

"Okay. No more running off in all directions, though. I want a solid plan."

"Yeah. We need our cats back. Both of them."

Brock needed to know James was going to heal.

Mick nodded, holding out a hand to shake. He got it. Mick needed to feel his skin, needed to seal a promise.

"My pack. All of you." The words sounded like a vow.

"Thank you." Griz meant it. He'd been a part of more than one team, but never part of a pack. Not ever. Something deep in his soul settled, going into hibernation. The pain of losing Brock the first time, maybe.

Rey came through with Dylan, humping computer and surveillance equipment like Mutt-and-Jeff pack mules.

"Boss?" Dylan stuck his head in the room. "We need to meet."

"Not until Kit gets back. Can you guys go get James? I want these two both in the same place."

"Yes." Rey nodded, and Griz had nothing but respect for the man. James had torn the hell out of the little fox and still, Rey was in.

"Thank you. I'm gonna go grab some printouts." Mick rose, heading out, which left Griz alone with Brock.

He got up so he could move to Brock's side. "Hang in there, kitty. You can't leave me now. I won't let you."

Brock groaned, tail lashing, moving furiously.

"I'm right here." He stroked that rough fur. "We're safe with the pack. James is coming to rest with you."

Griz thought his mate relaxed, eased down into the cot for him.

"Sweet kitty." God, his stomach was in knots. He wanted nothing more than for Brock to be awake, bitching at him, that gaze burning him to the ground.

Brock was strong. He would be fine. James was already recovering, right? Brock had the advantage that Kit knew what the poison was.

And his cat was strong. Brock wanted to come back to him.

Hell, he could hear the low mental *rowl*ing Brock was sending him now. Brock was hiding just below the surface.

The sedative was part of that, he knew. That would help slow the poison too, though.

He felt a brush along his spine, featherlight and teasing.

"Rest, baby. Rest. We're okay."

"Okay? Safe?"

"Yes. At a safe house with the pack." Griz would say pride, but Brock's kind of kitty was solitary, and it was a pack because Mick was the head, and he was a wolf.

"Pack." Obviously Brock understood, because he relaxed, the worry easing.

"Yes, love. Yes." He petted and praised, just losing himself for a moment.

"Stubborn, strong, beautiful mate."

"Mate." That sound in his head was satisfied.

Kit carried James in, the golden cat unconscious, limp. As soon as Kit set him down, Brock wrapped around him. Always protecting. Good man.

"Okay, Brock. I know you hate shots, but I have a dose ready for you." Kit kinda kept talking as he pushed the needle into Brock's leg.

Brock's yowl was sharp, complaining, but his mate didn't bite.

"That's it. I'll be back with another dose soon. More tailored to your poison." Kit stroked Brock's fur, then James's. "I got you, guys."

Griz nodded. "You do, brother. You do."

Kit reached out to him, so he grabbed Kit's hand. They needed it, both of them. The contact.

Pack. Somehow, someway, they were a crazy pack.

Griz felt totally humbled by their acceptance.

"Crazy, huh?" Kit touched his arm, a gentle smile on his face.

"Yes. I'm glad you're here, though. It's good to know another bear is here."

"It is. We're solitary, but somehow, it's so good to know someone understands."

Oh, Griz didn't think Kit was solitary at all. He thought the guy was lonely.

Lonely and desperately in love with his boss. Poor baby.

He shook his head. That wasn't his circus. And they had no monkeys in this pack.

Griz turned to his mate, sniffing to make sure Brock didn't smell like things were getting worse.

No. No, he thought the sour, sickly smell was fading.

"It's working much better on Brock, I think."

Griz nodded. "I bet it was the delivery. James got more, and he's smaller."

"And who knows how many doses, right?" Kit sighed and shook his head. "I know the boss will say my job is this, but what's the plan?"

"I have no idea. Mick is checking in with the wolf and fox about the weasel."

"Oh man. You have to start calling them by their names or we'll all get confused."

"I know. I know. Uh, Dylan and Rey." Griz snorted. "Don't know the weasel."

"We'll just call them poisonous assholes."

"I like it. I called an anaconda shifter that once. He happily informed me that snakes were venomous, and that he was not a viper. I told him I meant his farts." Griz thought some humor might help.

Kit chuffed softly, shoulders shaking as he fought his laughter. "Poots of Doom, eh?"

"Christ. He liked fish. A lot." He winked, knowing Kit probably liked a fish now and then, just like him. Maybe not as much as he craved salmon.

"Mmm.... Fish with blackberry cobbler for dessert."

"Yum. I can do a mean fish fry...." He was starving, suddenly.

"Yeah? Maybe after everyone's healed?"

"You know it." He would make Brock help. Kitty in an apron.

When Brock's lip curled, muzzle wrinkling, it soothed something deep down. He chuckled, stroking that heavy fur.

"Mate."

The thought suited him down to the bone. *"Yes. Mate. Finally."*

Now he just needed to make his lover well again and to solve this thing. Get who was doing this to them.

He had a feeling that would be easier said than done.

EIGHT

Brock felt as if he were underwater.

He could hear muffled voices, could feel the prick of a needle occasionally, but he couldn't seem to surface. *Merda*, he wanted to see Griz, to touch his mate and make sure he was okay.

He struggled, but the hands that landed on him calmed him.

"Sleep it off, mate. Kit is dosing you. You'll be fine."

"Mate. Griz. Love."

He wanted to wake up.

"Soon. James needs you. He's still not breathing well."

Okay. Okay, at least he had a job. He growled softly, reaching out to draw his brother in close, offering James his warmth.

Yes. He was getting better, because James felt solid, not far away. This he could do.

He could hear Mick and Kit talking, their voices familiar and deep, and when Griz answered? Well, that voice was burned into his soul.

Brock rested against James, gaining strength with each

minute. Sleeping in his cat form was always the easiest way to heal.

Hell, it was the easiest way to be, except for lovemaking. That could get awkward.

Griz was exponentially bigger in bear form, and then there was his cat's urge to defend itself.... Yeah, no.

Deep in his soul, he could feel his bear chuckling. *"Stoner kitty."*

"Shhh. Sleeping with someone else."

"I know. I'm jealous." That laughter helped heal him too.

"He's sexy, isn't he? Not as slinky as me, but...."

"He's sweet as candy, love. You're the sexy one." Griz stroked down his back, then tugged his tail.

A bright light slipped up along his spine, and he *rowl*ed.

"Did I hurt you?" Griz moved away a moment.

"No! No, you lit me up. Do the base of my tail?"

"Of course." Griz came close again, his warmth clear. Then Griz rubbed at the base of his tail, electrifying him.

He vocalized softly, letting Griz hear his happiness, the deep comfort.

"That's it, baby. Just rest and let me touch you." That deep mental rumble vibrated along his neck, and even James sighed, relaxing into him.

"Whatever you're doing, Locke, don't stop. It's helping." Kit sounded so pleased.

"I'm only loving on him. I wish—does James have anyone. Close?"

"No. I mean, Brock, of course. They're basically brothers." Kit sat nearby, sighed.

"Then it will help him to be here too." Griz petted him, loved him, still talking to Kit.

Brock focused on sending some of the love and energy to his best friend. James.

Of course it would help. James was family.

"That's it, guys. James, Griz says he'll do a fish fry if you wake up." Kit was excited by James's vitals, he could tell.

"Is Mick paying?" Brock asked.

"Yes." Griz sounded very sure about that. *"I haven't been paid yet."*

"Poor bear."

"Poor abused bear."

He did his best not to laugh, but Lord, he wanted to.

"I see you smiling, Brock," Kit said. "Griz is going to thump you, I bet."

"Nah, I'll wait until he's back in fighting trim," Griz murmured.

"Soon, I hope. I miss you both." Kit was a sweet, dear bear.

Brock wanted to tell him it would be all right, but wakefulness was still eluding him. Talking was too hard. He would let Griz share strength, then pass what he could on to James. Soon they would wake together.

"Shh... breathe, now. I'm right here." Griz kept talking, and he let himself float.

He just had to get through this. Then he could go back to kicking ass.

Brock chuckled, caressing Griz with his thoughts. The things he did to get a little rest.

———

"When the hell will they wake up?" Mick barked, making Kit look at him with a hurt expression. Poor kid. Mick was going to kick something, and Griz hoped it wasn't Kit.

"Brock's vitals are really good. I think he's waiting for James. Helping his energy levels."

"I need my team, Kit! I need to move on this before it's too late."

"I know! Okay, I get it." Kit blew out a sigh. "I also know this kind of toxin can damage liver and brain cells, and I want them healed."

"Boss, come on. Do you want me to get out there? Round up the client? I'll take Dylan with me." Griz needed Mick to calm down, focus.

"No. I want you all here, dammit."

"Okay." He held up his hands. "I'm right here."

"So are we." The fox, Rey, walked in, a tray in hand. "Coffee and stuff."

Dylan was right behind. "How're the cats? Any news? I'm ready to go kill something."

Mick growled lightly. "Me too. We just need to walk the line between getting out there and protecting the downed members of our pack. Without James's electronics...."

"I can try," Rey said. "I know I'm not James, but—"

"No, but we need eyes and ears. If you're willing." Mick perked up some.

"I can do it. I've been training."

"You gotta respect that, huh?" Griz liked the kid's gumption.

"Thanks. James always says we need cross-training."

"Huh." Mick snorted. "He never says it to me, kiddo. Okay, let's talk specs." They moved away, so Griz turned to Dylan and smiled.

"You need anything?" Dylan asked. "Coffee?"

"To rip someone's head off. Coffee works."

"Okay. I get you, man. When Rey was kidnapped—" Dylan grimaced. "—I was losing my mind."

"Yeah, at least I have Brock here with me."

"You do." Dylan looked down at Brock and James. "We need them."

"Yes." Goddess yes, with all his heart.

"They'll come around soon." Dylan reached out to touch James.

They'd better. Griz was getting impatient.

"Shhh. Waiting for James."

"Well, encourage him to surface."

"How?" Brock stretched, tail lashing.

"Wake up, baby. He'll follow you."

Those emerald eyes popped open, Brock ready to come back to the land of the living just like that.

"There you are." Thank God. Griz beamed, so happy it hurt.

Brock yawned and stretched, claws and fangs glinting. So pretty.

Griz rubbed that thick ruff, then scratched along Brock's back. "Better. So much better. Come on, James. We need you too."

Brock yowled and head-butted James, demanding attention.

One big, mountain lion paw came up, pushing at Brock's head.

Kit cheered. "James!"

James blinked awake, took a deep breath, then tried to stand up.

"No, no." Dylan jumped in to help ease James down. "Easy. You were poisoned."

Brock frowned, nosing James's back end. *"Mate? Something's wrong."*

"What? What's off?" His nose wasn't near as sensitive when he was a human, and to him the whole room smelled like sickness and antiseptic.

Brock sniffed and rumbled, nudging the golden back. *"Here."*

He bent to sniff, then looked at Kit. "Kit? James's back...."

Kit frowned, bent close. "James? Can you use your back legs? Move them?"

James scrabbled with his front feet, but no. Nothing in the back moved.

"Try again."

This time there was a weak, restless motion.

Kit pursed his lips. "Don't worry, buddy. This kind of toxin can leave some nerve damage, but you're a shifter. You'll heal." He sounded... not grim, but not happy. "It can take time."

"How much time?" Griz asked.

"Time."

"Oh." God, that sucked. He couldn't imagine not healing right up like all shifters.

Brock nosed his friend, a little trill coming from him.

James growled softly, and Brock wrapped around him, holding on with his huge paws. Yes. James would need reassurance, would need to keep from freaking out.

"We need to get him a doctor, Mick," Kit whispered. "A real one. Not just human EMTs. I know you hate to bring anyone in, but this is beyond me."

"Kiddo, you're a way better medic than you think, but I know someone who might be willing." Mick stepped out of the room, phone in hand.

Shit. Griz's heartbeat kicked into overdrive. Adrenaline.

"I'm going to kill them. All of them. I'll make them suffer." Brock sounded fierce.

"I'll help." His pack too now. His family.

"Yes." Brock stared at him in sheer fury. *"Together."*

Griz nodded grimly. Yes. They would all take vengeance for this.

Once they figured out if Hetrick was the only one behind this, at any rate. So goddamned frustrating, not being out there looking. He was an action guy, and his team had a lot of enemies.

"Me too. Let's go." Brock rolled up, teeth bared, hackles raised.

"Doc is on his way." Mick strode back into the room. "Not until I know you're in the clear physically, Brock."

"Bullshit. I'm out of here."

"Brock, you're a huge jaguar. It's noon. Someone will notice."

The wondrous part was that Mick knew exactly what Brock was thinking.

Those green eyes glowed with irritation, but Brock relaxed back down.

"Impressive, boss," Griz muttered.

"Lots of practice."

"I guess." It gave him a pang, how much he'd missed, how much he didn't know.

"Stop it. You know me at a cellular level."

"I know, baby. I missed stuff, is all. I love you." There was no blame there. The situation was what it was.

Brock swatted him playfully, the action kittenish and surprising. He laughed, delighted as hell.

"Seriously?" Mick pushed in and grabbed Brock, massaging him, loving on him.

Griz shook his head, just watching, proud of his lover for carving out a family, even when he was broken and wary.

"Come on, Brock. I'll watch James while you eat." At Brock's questioning *rowl*, Mick bared his teeth. "No one will get past me to him."

"I don't want to leave him, Mick." Griz made a point not to whine. He simply said it.

"I need you at strength."

Brock slowly shifted, looking pale and skinny, teeth and

claws too prevalent for too long. "Go get me a peanut butter sandwich, doof."

He laughed. "Okay. I'll save the fish fry for when James is up to it, huh?"

"When we're celebrating." His lover wore some brutal bruises.

"Yes." Griz bent to kiss Brock, then left the room. He needed to get them food, to honor Brock's effort in shifting with something good for him.

"Where are you going?" Rey stared at Brock, wide-eyed, as he tugged his clothes on. "Seriously, Brock. Where are you going?"

"Gonna get the client, honey, and then I'm going to bring him back here." They'd lollygagged long enough, dammit. No one seemed willing to commit to going after Hetrick, but how hard could he be to find?

"I'm coming with you."

"What?" He actually stopped and blinked over. "Nonsense. Dylan wouldn't let you."

"Locke won't let you. I can't let you go alone. We're pack."

"You're a fox." It was more of a tease these days, but when Rey's face fell, he reached out to touch. "I wasn't being ugly. I swear. I was trying to joke."

"But I know you had fox trouble."

"I had giant bleeding asshole trouble."

Rey giggled. There was no other word for it. *Adorable.*

"All right. You do James's job. I need your eyes, your help."

"Okay, but mobile surveillance is the way to go here so I can watch and listen and be the getaway driver." Rey was very, very serious.

"Fair enough. You ready?"

"Let's go. I've got your back. There's a van that's all tricked out and armed."

"Then let's go, buddy. We go bring his ass back."

They headed out, no one stopping them, which spoke to how distracted everyone was. No way would Griz let him go so soon, and Mick was losing it.

Good thing he knew where Stefan Hetrick lived, but the guy had to be too smart to be there. So, more importantly, he knew where Stefan's wife had her affairs, and they were going to start there. Hit the guy where it hurt.

"So, where do we begin?" Rey climbed into the van and pulled a laptop out from under the seat.

"We're going to the Moonlight Motel. That's the classy joint where Mrs. Hetrick has her affairs. The best way to trap a wolf is with fresh blood."

"Um. What are we using as bait? Not a fox, right?" Those glinting eyes glittered with laughter.

"Nope. We're going slinky kitty." He hoped that he still had a little slink left in him today.

"But you're not a hundred percent."

"Right, but his attacks centered on me and James. Kitty is what he wants."

"Okay... I have your back, man. I swear."

"Thanks." He gave Rey a wry smile. "If this goes *mau*, you run like hell. Get to Mick and Griz."

"Dylan will come for me, you know that."

"I know." He liked to think Griz would find him too, but he just wasn't sure of anything right now. Not only that, but he couldn't think about his mate yet. Not with the bond so fresh, so new. Not when he was doing something that would infuriate his bear.

He grinned a bit. Maybe Griz would try to spank him, and they could tear it up....

No. No thinking about Griz—especially like that.

"Focus," Rey chided gently. "Okay, tell me what you want me to do."

"We're going to the motel. Wifey wolf meets up with her favorite kitty every Thursday afternoon. As soon as we know she's checked in, we contact the mark." Hetrick obviously didn't want his wife's predilections made public, so that gave Brock the best chance to get the bastard out in public and alone.

Rey nodded. "Send him a picture and offer him a meet? That will keep any security at a minimum."

"You get me. Just like that. We'll use Griz's email to keep me out of it."

"Okay." Rey got typing. "I like it."

"Excellent." He wasn't sure how he was going to manage dealing with a wolf at full strength, but he'd figure that out there.

Maybe he'd try some of the same underhanded tactics Hetrick had used. Maybe he needed a tranq....

"Rey, when you're done, crawl in the back and see what we have as far as weaponry goes?"

"You bet. I need you to get me some pictures." Rey slid the laptop aside and popped into the back of the SUV.

"That shouldn't be a problem." At least he didn't think so.

"I know. I just mean I'm ready when we get there." The sound of rummaging reached him. "We have two handguns, a rifle, and three smoke grenades."

"No tranqs?" Dammit. Oh well, he could threaten with the best of them.

"The smoke grenades could work. There are some small breathers."

"Good deal." The tiny gas masks did enough to keep the invader's eyes and nose clear. "That'll work in a pinch."

They pulled into the parking lot, and he eased the vehicle around behind.

"Okay, I got your back." Rey climbed over the seats again, armed to the teeth.

"That's sexy, fox." He winked, letting Rey know the tease was gentle.

"Thanks." Rey posed à la the raccoon in the *Galaxy* movie thingees. "All right, go forth and get me dirt. Be careful."

"Dirt is my specialty." He slipped out of the truck, heading to room 105, the one with the broken blind. He stayed in the shadows, slinking along and staying low to the ground.

He might not be in kitty form, but he was a cat no matter what.

The scent of sex was heady on the air, even through the glass, and he peeked in to see the wolf and cat going to town. Not bad at all. All he had to do was get his phone out to get some graphic pics.

One, two, three. He got the images, and as he went for the fourth, the bobcat looked right into the lens.

Motherfucker.

Hank Delong. Undercover cop, and this lady wolf was so not his jam.... So he had to be on a sting.

He smiled and did his best to slink away, which would be easy, except that was the moment Griz discovered he was gone....

"Brock!" The mental shout made his eyes cross.

"La la la. Busy busy. Working." He sent a wave of love and kept moving.

He had to get back to Rey and then somehow send a message to Hank to get lost. With his luck, Hank would contact Mick. What a clusterfuck.

Rey held a hand out for his phone as soon as he got back in the SUV. "How did it go?"

"Don't ask. Dylan know you're gone?"

Rey held up his phone with ten missed calls. "Uh-huh."

"Oops. There's a cop in there." They were so screwed. He could either go forward and blow Hank's plan or retreat and come up with something else.

"Oh, that's probably bad, huh?"

"Probably."

"Where the fuck are you?"

"Working. At the hotel where the Stefan Hetrick guy's wife is fucking an undercover cop bobcat named Hank."

"Hank Delong?" That mental shout rose in volume. A lot.

"Shh. Busy. I'll be back... shortly." Did lying work like this?

"Goddammit, kit."

Rey's phone started vibrating. He didn't even glance at it. "Typing!"

"Fuck, fuck!" *What to do, what to—* "What can you tell me about Hank Delong? Hurry."

"Hank Delong? D-e-l-o-n-g?" Rey typed faster than anyone he'd ever met. "No longer with the police department. Ties to DEA and FBI. Supposedly went rogue last year in a very public falling out."

"Ah. Okay." He wouldn't risk another cop's life. He couldn't.

"So, what now?"

"Now I call the boss. Dammit." He hated when he had to be all rule-following.

"It's about time."

"Shut up."

Brock was about to call Mick when Hank came slinking out, eyes searching the parking lot for them.

He pushed a hand out the window, signaling from where they perched on the end, almost the corner.

Hank lifted his chin, before getting in a vehicle and starting the engine.

"We're going to follow him, Rey. Right now, stick with the plan."

"Are you sure?"

Not even a little bit. "Totally."

"But Mick...."

"We follow Hank." Hank wouldn't be on the wrong side of this. He wouldn't. "Once I go to Hank, you call Mick. Fair?"

"Only if I can monitor you with a mic." Rey got a stony look.

"Works for me. Get it set up." He was stubborn, not stupid.

"Cool." Rey dragged a suitcase out from under a seat. "Mick has the best toys."

"James has everything organized to death." The words *James* and *death* in the same sentence made him wince.

Rey glanced up, eyes shadowed with worry. "He's recovering."

"Slower than I like." He followed Hank, the low-slung black sports car Hank drove easy to keep in view.

"Yes, he had a way bigger dose, but you got your ass kicked, so...."

"I will bite you, fox."

"Promise?" Rey batted his eyelashes.

"No biting the fox...."

"He's mated."

"So are you." The grizzly growl was so hot.

"Working. Hush."

A soft chuckle trailed after him. *"Be careful."*

He fully intended to do so. He just needed to figure out what was up.

As soon as Hank parked and ducked inside a door at the end of a strip mall, Rey hooked him up with a mic. "Okay, go get him, panther."

"Rawr." He brushed his hand through his hair and sighed. "Be back." Hopefully.

"I'm listening." Rey tapped his headphones.

"Thanks. Record everything. If Hank jams me, call our mates."

"I will, I swear. No more dangling team members." Rey sounded deadly serious. Good man.

He had the sinking suspicion Dylan and Griz were on their way anyway. The way Rey pursed his lips, head tilting, told him the same thing.

"Yeah. Stall them." He hopped out and jogged toward the doorway, refusing to let Hank see him sweat.

"Gotcha," Rey called softly, and the door shut behind him.

Hank opened the door when Brock reached it, stepping back to let him in.

He slid in, entire body ready to attack.

"What the fuck, man? Are you trying to blow my cover?" Hank slammed the door shut.

"What are you doing humping a married woman?" he shot right back.

"Shit, man, you know normally I don't hump women at all." Hank sighed. "I'm on assignment."

"You think? What's up, bud? Seriously, what is going on with this? Her husband tried to kill me."

"Oh, man, this is a Pandora's box of fuck-upped-ness." Hank waved him to a chair. "What isn't this guy into?"

"Apparently guys." He tried for a wry grin and almost made it.

"No, that he's not into, or I'd be humping him." Hank flipped him off. "I'm looking into a drug operation he's running."

"A... a what?" Maybe he'd misunderstood. There was a

cult or something, weasels poisoning people, and a cheating wife, but drugs too? *Jesus*.

"Drug operation. Cocaine mainly." Hank sighed. "That's not what my bosses are interested in, though. They're looking for a new synthetic on the market—Peaches."

"Peaches? What the hell is that?" Brock felt completely off-kilter. "What the *fuck* is that?"

"A hallucinogen. Some say mind control."

"And it's synthetic?" He was pretty sure Kit had said the poison compound he and James had been hit with was organic....

"That's the rumor. You have other information?" Those blue eyes went sharp fast.

"I don't know. One of our guys got hit by a poisonous attack at the office. Our med tech thinks it's plant-based, though."

"Have him check out this Peaches. Maybe someone mixed it with another compound. Maybe it wasn't this guy." Hank tilted his head. "What are you after him for?"

"The wolf with the wife? Cult. Weasels. Poison. You name it."

Hank's mouth dropped open, then closed, then opened again. "Pardon?"

Brock held out a hand to tick off points. "I told him yes, his wife was cheating. He hit me. Griz took over the case. We were attacked. The office was infiltrated by weasels, who poisoned James, which led us to a cult hanging out in a warehouse. Got it all?"

"Uh-huh." Hank tilted his head. "Griz as in Locke the bear?"

"Yep." He would not blush or look away.

"Huh. Interesting. Very interesting."

He wasn't here to talk about Griz. "Yeah, well, I need a sample of this Peaches shit."

"And I need you to back off the missus." Hank didn't look like he was joking.

"I can't. You know that." Brock had a job to do. "She's connected to a man I gotta find."

"And I can't let you fuck up my investigation." Hank actually looked sorry. "I think she's going to invite me to the house, let me see her pool."

"You have to watch yourself, Hank. He'll just poison you eventually. You gotta get out of this." Brock felt that deep down.

"I do, but I got a job, exactly like you do."

"So tell them the wife is an exhausted source."

"I need a few days, man. Back off for a few days, and I'll get you a sample."

Brock shook his head, frustration flooding him. "I don't have—"

"Brock! Brock, help!"

The cry through the earpiece had him jumping to his feet. "Rey."

"Huh?"

"Outside! He's in the van. My backup." He ran, because Rey wouldn't sound the alarm for no reason.

Hank's footsteps were right behind him, chasing him, running with him.

He didn't yell out; he waved to Hank to flank the van.

A short nod was his only answer. Brock didn't bother with the throat mic. The earpiece had gone dead. Hand on his sidearm, he slowed, creeping to the open van door.

"Griz. Griz, hurry. Bring backup."

"Brock? We're coming! Rey sent us coordinates! Be careful." Griz sounded frantic.

"Hurry!" Brock pushed into the van, pistol drawn.

"Empty," Hank said from the passenger side.

He glanced over, eyes going wide as the cop's face disappeared under a black sack. "Fuck!"

Brock turned to run, to try to find a way to help Hank and Rey, but it was too little too late. A needle plunged deep into his arm, and damn if the whole fucking world didn't go black.

NINE

"*Hurry!*"

Griz heard that and then nothing but a pure silence.

"Goddamn it!" he roared.

"Now! In the car!" Mick shoved him, Dylan ahead of him and jumping into the driver's seat.

"They've got Rey," Dylan barked. "What the fuck was Brock thinking?"

"Shut up. Just drive." Mick growled the words furiously. "Get the small arms together, Locke."

"I'm driving! That's my mate!" Dylan sounded like he was about to shatter into a thousand pieces.

"He's fine. They'll both be fine." Griz said it, but his lips felt numb, and there was a blank spot in his brain where Brock should be.

Dylan shot him a glare, but he knew that Dylan understood. They had to find their mates. Now.

"Why the hell did they sneak off?" Mick snapped.

"They were just gathering intel." Griz didn't really get it either.

"Was he in his right mind? I mean, the poison."

"Maybe not." God, why wouldn't Brock wake up? He had to be unconscious. Griz would know if— *No. No way.*

"Rey would go with him, to protect him." Dylan sounded so sure.

"I know. He's a good guy." The whole team was full of them. They had Brock's back.

"So is Brock. Stubborn. Aggravating. Mulish." Dylan grinned over. "But good."

"Yeah. Mine." Damn it.

Mick snorted. "He is. That's weird, you know?"

"Bears are the best, just ask me."

He got this odd look from Mick. "I like them okay."

"Boss, I'm not asking you to mate with me. I like pussy."

"That was bad." Mick turned, shook his head. "How are we armed?"

"Well. We have five handguns with plenty of ammo, three rifles, and a handful of flash bangs. Whoever maintains the vehicles...."

"Carrie does that," Dylan murmured.

"She fucking rocks, man."

"She does. That's why it's so hard that she goes to keep her mom safe whenever we lock down." Mick winked broadly. "We're getting close to the last known location."

Griz smelled the smoke before he saw it, acrid and bitter on his nose. His eyes watered a little, but that was nothing to what happened to his heart when he saw what was burning. The van. It had to be the van Brock and Rey had taken.

"No." Dylan's voice was black, more a snarl than a word.

"Stop." The order came as a roar, and Dylan obeyed his pack leader, stopping a safe distance from the van.

Griz was less willing to listen. He growled, reaching for the door.

Mick snapped, and he could feel claws on his arm. "I go first. Stay here."

Then Mick was off and running.

He chafed, but he was part of a team again, and he needed to wait. Brock wasn't here. He wasn't in that van.

"They weren't in there," he grumbled.

"Locke...."

"They weren't fucking in there!"

Dylan nodded miserably. "Okay. Okay. I'm going into the building, see what I can see."

"I can do that." When Dylan *grrr*ed at him, he shook his head. "As a bear, I can take ten small caliber bullets before I even slow down. Can you?"

"Fuck you. That's my mate that was in there!"

"And we have to work together to get them back!" He grabbed Dylan, shook him. "Our mates. Those are our mates."

"I know. Go! I'll lay down cover fire if you need it." He could see the agony on Dylan's face.

"Just leave one alive." He needed to know where his kit was.

"I will." He would get in and get out. Hell, there might not be anyone in there. At least he knew Hank and wouldn't shoot on sight. He couldn't say the same of Dylan.

Weapon at the ready, he made a mad rush into the building, the scent of the burning van dominating but hints of Brock right there.

Okay. Okay. "Mate? Are you here? Wake up!"

He got no answer; the place was deserted. Nothing. No one.

It was just... an empty warehouse. What the fuck? Why did they come here? He checked his danger areas, and even the back entrance, hunting any clue.

That was when he saw the edge of a manila envelope, slid under an empty file cabinet.

Score. Well, as long as it wasn't someone's light bills or something. Griz grabbed it up and thumbed it open.

There were photos of Hetrick and his wife, inventory sheets with Hetrick's name on them, an article on a new street drug. Nothing at all about a cult.

Damn. The drug angle might be something.... Who called anything Peaches?

This was not a macho drug name. Not at all.

Maybe that was the point. Make it sound innocuous.

There was something else in the file, though. A new address for Hetrick, one out in Evergreen he'd never seen before. A surge of satisfaction roared through him even as caution warned him to wonder why the information was just lying around. He headed back out to the SUV at a trot, making sure he wasn't reckless.

"Anything?" Mick asked. "The van is wiped out. Nothing there."

"Just this." He handed over the folder. Mick was the boss.

Mick read, flipping with a speed that left him breathless. "We need to get this to Kit, but first, we're going to pay a visit to our client."

"Good." Dylan slapped his hand on the steering wheel. "Let's go."

That was the first really good idea anyone had had all fucking day. He took back the folder. "I'll send pics to Kit on the way."

"Perfect. Tell him to look at that Peaches shit."

"You got it." Maybe that could help James. He needed the distraction or he'd go mad.

"What's the plan, boss?" Dylan asked.

"I talk. You're my heavies. If he bolts, you two take his ass down."

"You got it." With pleasure. "No killing him until we know where our mates are."

"That will be up to you, boys." Mick's grin was deadly.

"Then not until we know," Dylan agreed, eyes flashing gold.

No one—crocs, snakes, wildebeests—no one could have their mates again. He knew Dylan agreed.

Mick skidded through a series of twists and turns, but it surprised him how close the client really was to their previous location, and to the warehouse he and Brock had visited.

"Locke, I need to know if you smell Rey here," Mick barked as soon as he parked.

He lifted his head, closing his eyes to channel the one sense. "No." No Brock either.

"Okay, so no one came here. Let's go find out where they took them." Mick's eyes glowed in the cab.

He and Dylan nodded, just... yeah. They would beat it out of the son of a bitch if they had to.

Armed and dangerous, they swarmed out of the SUV, moving like they'd been working together for ages. He got these people; they were Brock's pack, and now his. Family.

"This is no residence." Dylan held up a hand, stopping them all. "Chemicals?"

Mick nodded. "He owns this building. His office is here."

Dylan passed out face masks, and Griz put his on with a snarl. He hated this shit. Still, he wasn't going to end up like James. He needed to find his mate, and he needed to do this with a clear head.

They hit the door in unison, popping the lock and backing off as the flash-bang went off.

"All good?" Mick snarled.

"Yes, sir." Dylan was already moving in under the smoke, weapon drawn.

"Clear!" Dylan's voice carried despite the distorting mask.

Griz ducked into the building, searching for any movement not Dylan's.

He knew they weren't alone. Even if the door had been booby trapped, everything inside him insisted that this was wrong.

"Watch your six," Mick barked, telling Griz he wasn't just imagining it.

"On it."

Dylan moved first, low and quick, trying to flush out whoever was hiding into the light.

A loud grunt sounded, and someone ran into Dylan, knocking him aside. Dylan went flying actually, so someone was either in wolf-change or hyped on drugs or something.

One way or the other, Locke was a motherfucking grizzly in his prime and pissed off. He won.

He growled, letting the bear fill him. He couldn't shift all the way, not and keep his weapon out of enemy hands, or breathe, but the strength moved in him.

Without a single hesitation, he rushed the bastard, his bear driving him forward, demanding satisfaction.

Dylan flanked him, coming in fast from the side, driving the man-wolf back toward the corner of the room with no doors or windows.

"I'd surrender, if I were you, Hetrick. My pack is not pleased." Mick's voice was dry as dust.

The urge to destroy the fucker was huge, and only the knowledge that they had Brock stopped him. He needed this one to tell him where.

"Grab the bastard!" Mick roared as soon as Hetrick's arms raised in defeat, so they did. Locke on one side, Dylan on the other.

Dylan's eyes glowed softly, fury dripping from the wolf. "Where are they?"

A mouthful of razor sharp teeth opened. "Fuck off."

Mick's chuckle was possibly the scariest thing he'd ever heard. "Are you very sure about that, my friend?"

"Yes." The rattle when Mick reached out to squeeze the guy's throat was awesome.

"Shall we start by ripping off his dick?"

"Please, boss." Dylan growled, and Griz agreed completely.

"Good deal." Mick ripped the guy's pants down.

"Motherfuckers!"

"You'll need a strap-on in three, two...." Griz was ready.

"No!" The howl told them Mick had read their former client correctly. Asshole lived by his dick.

"Where. Is. My. Mate?" He ripped open the bastard's unders.

"In another property of mine." Those eyes were really bugging out now.

"Do better. The boys are hungry."

Dylan let himself smile, the grin pure evil, and pure teeth.

"Christ. It's in Aurora." The sweat that poured off the man was pure desperation. "Take off the masks so I can see your faces at least."

"Not a chance." Griz snarled. The guy had to know who he'd crossed, yeah?

"Fucking cats." The man spat the words. "A fucking blight."

Before he could roar, Mick picked the guy up and slammed him on the ground with a bone-breaking sound. "My *pack*!"

Coughing, then moaning, the asshole nodded. "Aurora." He rattled off an address, not even a real challenge.

"Put him in the vehicle. Tie his ass up good. We're heading to Aurora."

"You got it, boss." He and Dylan made quick work of it, using zip ties from the SUV.

"Let's do this. It's time to go find the boys."

Who the hell knew what they would find, but they had to try. This was the best lead they could get.

———

"Brock. Brock, kitty, please! Please, you got to wake up. They've tied me up."

Brock tried to lift his head, but it was so damn heavy. He could hear the voice, but.... But damn.

"Brock! Goddamn it, wake your ass up!"

He blinked. That was also familiar, but not Mick. Not Griz.

"They think you're out for the count. The cop is still out. I'm in a cage, buddy. Please."

"Rey?" he croaked the name, because it was fox he heard, smelled.

"Yes. Yes, thank Goddess. Yes. Please, man. You have to get up. They poisoned you and the cop. I think Kit's medicine was still in you."

"Oh...." He blinked. Sure enough, it was Rey. "You?"

"I'm only little. No threat, right?" Rey's eyes shone.

"Right." Good man. Rey could go limp and boom. He would look like a kid to these guys.

"I figured one of us needed to wake up. Dylan is coming. Get me out."

"Mate!" Griz's call almost knocked him down.

"Ow." He fought back a grin. His mate was agitated. "Get you out of what?"

"The cage, Brock. Pay. Attention."

"I'm trying, man. I am." He shook his head. How was he contained? Was he?

"I know. It's hard. Your hands are tied, but if you don't struggle you can slip out."

"Okay." He licked his lips, his tongue feeling fuzzy. "Calm. No struggling." He went kitty limp, willing his hands to slip out of the bindings.

If Rey hadn't warned him, he would have pulled, but instead he eased one hand out.

"Smart fox." He did grin now. *"One hand free, love."*

"I'm coming for you. Going to kill someone."

"Promise?" He rolled up to all fours, panting as if he was the wolf. Okay. He could do this. All he had to do was open Rey's cage.

"You have my word. Get ready."

"Let me get Rey free." Brock's whole body felt stupid, clumsy. "Dylan and Griz are coming. We need to get you out."

"I think this is a great goddamn plan, buddy."

He *rowl*ed out a laugh, because Rey sounded so much like Mick or Dylan—very hard-boiled. Not like him at all.

Rey winked at him. "Am I doing a great job of hiding my terror?"

"You are! I'm very proud." He hauled himself up by grabbing the cage Rey sat in.

"Excellent. Can you break the lock?"

"I dunno, kiddo." He peered at it, willing his eyes to work. "Griz could."

"Okay." Rey settled in the back corner of the cage, head on his knees.

"No, I can try. I'm sorry, Rey. I'm just moving slow." God, what the hell was this shit they were poisoning him and James and now Hank with? Christ. He took a deep breath. Then another. It would really help to have Rey free when their mates showed.

"It sucks. No one thinks I'm dangerous."

Brock knew better, though. "I know now, kiddo." Okay. "Did they search me?"

"No. They wanted out of here, to call their leader."

"So the cult guys took us?" He searched his pockets. He had matches in a waterproof container, and he hoped he still had a few rounds from a revolver he'd been using for shooting practice... whatever day he'd put on these pants.

"Yeah. I think the drug guy and the cult guy are the same guy."

"I think I know who that is." He winked. Score. Okay, now. The lock wasn't exactly crap, but this would work if he could steady his fingers.

"I can smell the powder." Rey looked fascinated. "You'll teach me this?"

"I will." He would teach Rey all kinds of things. For a fox, he was damned cool.

"Thank you. I hear voices coming."

"Shit. Shit, okay." All right. They would hear the lock blow. *Come on, Griz. They're coming.* Brock shook his head, trying to get his shit together. "Can you hear what they're saying?"

"They... they can't get hold of their grand high pooh-bah. They don't know what to do."

"Good. Confusion is good." That would give them the edge, maybe enough to get them out, and get Hank help.

"Yeah, for them, not for us."

"You got it. Get back, Rey."

"Almost there" came Griz's mental voice.

Rey scrambled to face the back of the cage, arms up to cover his head.

"So are they, mate."

Brock lit the match, setting it to the little fuse he'd made from a piece of his shirt. "Fire in the hole!"

Rey cowered a bit more into his arms, and after a second, the lock blew with a sharp snap.

"Come on, foxy. Help me get Hank." Brock swung open the gate.

"I'm on it. They're close. They're coming." Rey moved like lightning, heading to snap Hank's bonds.

"So are Griz and Dylan." Meanwhile, he slogged as if he was stuck in feijoada.

"I know. Come here and get behind me." Little Rey puffed up and tried to seem big.

Brock wasn't about to laugh. "No, I get in front, and you push me like a puppet." He could seem huge, and he knew it.

"I promise to take care of you. I will fight too." Rey bared sharp needle-like teeth.

"I know you will. I trust you with my back."

The door burst open, and it was go time. They couldn't carry Hank, not like this, so they had to fight until Griz and Dylan and Mick came.

"What are you doing, asshole?" There were four of them —all wolves, all strung out so far they shook. Looked like the cult was fed a lot of whatever drug Hetrick was pushing now. Coke? Peaches? Jesus.

"Leaving." He said it like he meant it.

"No. How the fuck did you get loose?"

"I'm magic, you fucker."

Rey was the magic one. Maybe foxy could run.

"Hold on, mate. Hold on."

"Hurry. I can't keep this up." His head was spinning, and Rey was half holding him up.

"Let them get closer, then cover your ears, okay?"

"Huh?" He had no idea what Rey had planned, but he could do that. In fact, he could draw them in.

"I can scream like a banshee, and they are close to running now."

"Shit. Right." He beckoned. "Come on, dipshits. Come get me."

"We're keeping you for our master...," one of the creeps muttered.

"Master schmaster." He let out a string of Portuguese, hoping to unnerve them.

"Hitting the door."

"Now, Brock," Rey whispered.

Brock fell to his knees, clapping his hands over his ears as he went down. *"Rey is screaming!"*

The sound stopped the entire world for a second, stealing sound and color away, and when it stopped, Griz was there.

"Come on, baby. Time to go."

"Hank—"

"Mick has him." Griz jerked his chin, and sure enough, Hank was bouncing on Mick's shoulder.

He stayed right on Griz's side, using the huge man's strength to support him. His feet tried to tangle, and Dylan flew past with Rey in his arms.

Brock thought Rey could probably go on his own steam.... "What's wrong with Rey? What about the wolves?"

"We have their Alpha."

"Oh, well, that's helpful." Brock fought the urge to giggle.

"Hold it together, mate. Rey is out cold. A dart, I think."

"Trying. I want to go home, Griz."

"I know. Come on, baby. Come on."

They staggered out to the SUV, Mick shoving Hank in the back.

Man, if wolfboy back there knew Hank was humping his wife to get information on his drug business, he'd be pissed. More than now, even. What a fucking mess.

"He'll be coming after Hank, for sure." Griz helped him into the vehicle.

"You have him, right? Hank can deliver his skanky ass to his bosses."

"Yep." Mick snarled the word. "Then we find out what the hell is going on with this shit substance so no one can use it on us."

"Kit's on the right track. Brock doesn't seem affected nearly as much as the cop." Dylan wouldn't let go of Rey's hand.

"Good. Good." Mick climbed into the driver's seat. "Hold on."

He nodded, closed his eyes, and leaned into Griz.

"I got you. I do."

Griz had better, because he couldn't hold himself up anymore. His head felt so heavy, and his stomach roiled.

"Gonna be sick." Brock knew he wouldn't if he could help it, but he thought it wise to warn.

"Breathe, mate." A window opened, the icy air making it better.

"Thank you. *Deus.*" His English did try to abandon him when he was in extremis.

"You're welcome, kit. Breathe. In and out."

"Breathing." In and out. He could do it. He could.

"When we get back, we'll go away for a few weeks. Relax. Eat."

"Please. Fuck, yes." He could so get away with his mate and cement the bond.

"Good food, rest, a ton of sex."

A chuckle escaped him, because right now the very thought made his head ache.

"Hey, a bear can fantasize, can't he?"

"I can promise way more than a fantasy once I get over whatever the hell this is."

"TMI," Mick barked.

"He's got no sense of humor, eh?"

"Mate loneliness." There was a story there, but Brock had no idea what it was. It was none of his, was it? His job was to defend Mick as the pack member he was.

Griz frowned. *"That sucks for him."*

Brock nodded. They both knew the pain of mating issues.

"He'll find the one. You did."

"And he finally came back to me." Griz held him close, and the nausea finally faded completely, leaving him drained.

"There we go, kit. That's better."

"Thank you." He glanced at Hank, who was gray and barely breathing. "He needs help, Mick. Hurry."

"Kit's waiting with the antidote for him and you and Rey, just in case." Mick revved the engine and sped up.

"'M okay," Rey murmured, rousing a bit. He really sounded out of it. That was probably bad.

"Don't you die, fox. You owe me."

"Uh-hunnn. My tongue feels funny." Rey's tongue sounded funny too.

"Alpha!" Dylan sounded utterly desperate. "*Please.*"

"Two minutes. Call Kit. Have him meet us outside. We can't wait to get them in." Mick's voice was guttural. Harsh.

"I'm on it." Griz had his phone in his hand.

Good man. He leaned down, clinging to Griz with one hand, touching Rey with the other. "I'm serious, fox. You hold on." His world began to get fuzzy around the edges.

"I got this," Rey murmured. It was adorable and maddening at the same time.

The big SUV skidded to a stop, the smell of burning rubber huge. They must be there. Here.

Whatthefuckever.

"Kit! Help them!" His roar didn't sound nearly as loud as he'd expected.

"I'm here." The door flew open, Kit there like some comic book hero, pusher with needles bristling from his fingers.

"Wow." There just wasn't anything else to say. "Rey first, then Hank."

"I won't forget you, Brock. Rey, I need your belly. That will be the fastest."

Dylan tore at Rey's shirt, baring his concave stomach. "Please."

"He'll be fine, Dylan. You have my word."

Brock closed his eyes, the world going distant, fuzzy. "Me last," he reminded them.

"Shut up," Griz said. He felt the sting of a needle sliding into his skin only moments later. Looked like Kit was in super-human speed mode.

"Inside," Mick barked. "We'll put them with James."

"James is up. He's all kitty, but he's up."

Oh, thank the Goddess. That was a huge improvement, and it gave him hope for Hank, who was still dead to the world.

"Rey said they didn't drug him...."

"Swell, Rey was wrong, mate. They poisoned him. Breathe. Relax. You're fine."

"Air... but it's okay for you to breathe my air?" Brock thought that was important.

"I swear. Breathe, pretty kitty."

"Okay. Okay." He floated, and he knew Griz was carrying him, taking him to safety. His family. God, this was a mess. Someone really had it in for them.

Brock tried to shake his head, but it just wouldn't cooperate. *"Griz. Love."*

"Rest. I'll watch over all of you. Then we'll discuss this whole sneaking off thing."

"Hmm?" It was hard to do innocent when you were stoned.

"You heard me, kit. I love you."

"Love you...." His body landed on a bed, and everything that was clenched relaxed a tiny bit. Oh, maybe he could simply sleep. Hank. Rey. They would be okay now.

A rough tongue began grooming him, the scent of James sudden and welcome. Brother.

Oh, it was good to know James was awake. When had he shifted, Brock had no idea. Still, he was ready to let Griz take the wheel for a bit, so to speak.

His bear could carry him.

TEN

"Okay, I am sick of this shit, Mick." Griz hurt. All over. He was exhausted, and his mate was out like a light. "I want this over."

"You and me both, man. I'm going to have to call the cops soon, turn this asshole over." Mick looked livid as fuck.

"I know, but we need information first. The cops won't share much, will they?"

"They did okay with Patel," Mick said, referring to the tiger who'd killed their last office building. "You can go see what you can get out of him, but we're running out of time."

"Okay. I'll try it." Griz would bear out maybe. Scare the guy. He was the apex predator here.

Without his pack, the guy had zero chance. Hell, Griz wasn't even sure the asshole had a pack. A cult of scared, skinny wolves was more... henchmen who would turn on him.

Griz headed off to the containment room Mick had set up.

It was a damn good thing he was ready, because the motherfucker launched himself at Griz as soon as the door opened.

That was a shitty idea.

He roared, lunging to smack the guy down. "I don't think so."

This motherfucker had tried to kill his mate.

Twice.

Griz shoved the guy down, then put a foot on his throat. "Stay down."

Claws scrabbled at his boots, but they couldn't get through the leather. Not wolf claws. Now, Brock would have shredded him. He grinned at the thought.

"I said stay. Tell me where you're manufacturing the drugs. Why did you attack us? What the fuck is going on?"

The wolf struggled, choking sounds coming through, so Griz eased up a quarter of an inch.

"F-fuck you."

"Not an option, dickmunch."

"Get off!" The guy was more guy and less wolf every second.

"Answer my question." He could stand there forever.

"You're trying to shut down my operation. Working with the fucking cop!"

"You hired us, dickhead." It was an important distinction.

"Shut up! To follow my wife, not to ruin me. I didn't know you were in league with the cops. And I was told—" Hetrick cut the words off, eyes shifting side to side, those hands working at Griz's leg again.

"We were following your wife, or so we thought. We were trying to get pictures of her fucking one of your managers."

"Let me go!" The guy went wild, the wolf coming back to the fore.

"What? It pisses you off that the missus was getting bobcat tail?"

"Fucker!" Lord, this one was crazy as a bedbug. And full of weird contradictions.

"What's with the fucking psychos, man? What's with the weasels?" He was fixin' to lose his temper.

"It's the new drugs. They make everyone nuts."

He thought maybe that was the first honest thing Mr. Wolf had said.

"Nuts and willing to obey your skanky ass for more?" Made him wonder if the missus hadn't tried it.

"Yes. Yes, okay? It makes them weak-willed." A huge gasp of air came when Griz lifted his foot a little more.

"And you poisoned us because...?"

"To get rid of you." The guy went limp, flopping down. "To get rid of the threat."

"Dude, you're kinda stupid. You couldn't have just fired us?"

"Like that asshole feline would have let my drug operation at the warehouse go? What a fucking mess."

Okay, in that he might have a point.

Griz wasn't sure which feline he meant, though. Brock or Hank? They hadn't even known about Hank....

"You're not working for anyone else?" Griz bore down again.

"The whole point of manufacturing is that you're not, dickweed." But Hetrick's heart rate went way up, the smell of stress sweat suddenly twice as strong.

"So they say." Druggies were always interconnected. "Don't lie to me, man. Just a bad idea. I'm a bear shifter."

"There are scarier things in the world than you, asshole."

So he was working for someone. Maybe someone who was calling the shots, which would explain why Hetrick sent them to the warehouse even if he didn't want them to find his drug ring. "Yeah. Crocodile shifters." *Bleh.* "But not for you. Not right now."

"You got me, okay? Call the fucking cops. They'll be pleased to have me out of the way. So will the wife."

"You got it." He whirled, headed for the door, and managed to leave before the asshole could even get up.

Mick was waiting for him, arms crossed over his chest. "Well?"

"Swears it's all because we stumbled on his drug op." There was more going on, but the cops would have to go after that information, right? They were just PIs, damn it, not black ops or undercover agents, and they'd suffered too much for this case.

"No fucking way." The wolf flared in Mick's eyes. "No. Fucking. Way."

"He's more scared of someone else than he is of us, man. We need Hank and Brock awake. We all need to compare notes." Somewhere he had a feeling they had the answers and didn't know it.

"I can't hold him until then. He'll claim kidnapping."

"He wants the cops. Like Patel. Remember how he went willingly at the end? Like they were both more scared of something other than us." Griz spread his hands. "What the fuck, Mick?"

"I don't know, but I'm going to find out, I swear to you." Mick growled and put his fist through the wall. "Dammit!"

He raised his eyebrows. "Is this a rental?"

"I know the owner." Mick glared at him. "Go see your cat, asshole. I'll see what else I can get out of him."

"Going." He'd done part of the job. If Mick wanted a crack at the guy, maybe he could use his wolfiness to an advantage. Griz needed to see Brock.

Some things were more important. He needed his kit.

"Hey, baby." Griz slid into the bed on the opposite side of James, who was still all wrapped up with Brock. Warm kitties.

"Oh, love. I dreamed you left."

"Never. Went to interrogate the wolf dickhead. Worthless piece of shit."

"What did you find out? Anything good?"

"Swears it's about the drugs." Griz closed his eyes to breathe in that amazing musky scent.

"Fucking drugs. Never again. Not me or James or Rey or you."

"No. I'm okay. We're all gonna be okay."

"You sorry you came for me?"

"What? No. Never. I love you." He meant it with his whole soul.

Brock snorted, hiding in James's pelt, holding himself carefully stiff.

"Are you—" He bit the words off out loud. *"Are you worried you made a mistake taking me back?"*

"No. You're my bear. Mine." Those green eyes flashed at him.

"Oh good." He kissed Brock's ear, making it flick, tickling his lips. *"Silly kitty."* His heart felt so damn full. Jesus, what a day.

"Tell me about our vacation."

"Mmmm. We could go to the mountains. Sit in a hot tub and drink hot buttered rum. Nap a lot. Or we could go to the beach and bake you like a clam, laze around with umbrella drinks."

"Or both. I don't mind hot tubs at all."

"Me either." The mountains first, then. Snow. Naps. Fires. Bubbles.

A huge bed. One that could take their combined weight. As animals. Oh, that would be awesome. He might have to think about buying a place. Well, once he had some cash.... God.

"I have a place for us, mate. A place for bears."

"You do?" Brock had that amazing house, but it wasn't exactly a cabin in the woods.

"What do I have to spend money on but hideaways?"

"Mmm." He loved the idea of discovering all these weird places Brock had bought all over the place. He stroked that long back. *"Doesn't it bother you that I'm a broke soldier of fortune?"*

"You're mine. I need you, Paddy."

"Shhh." He chuckled, that name making him do it every time. Lord.

Green eyes stared at him. *"It's time for us to go away, bear. I'm tired."*

"I hear you." He got it. Brock had been through a lot. His team had been through it too.

It was time to leave this behind for a while, spend some time alone, quiet. Together.

"Hey. James. Can I borrow you?" Kit's voice was quiet, low, and he eased James away from them.

Brock immediately leaned into Griz, soaking up his strength.

"I got you, baby. I do. We'll wrap this case up and go away. I swear."

Brock nodded, groaning softly as he tried to relax. Those poor muscles were so sore. So still. Griz could feel it.

"Hold me." The command was sure, needy, aching.

"I have you." He did, wrapping his arms around his mate so tight.

Brock went boneless, trusting him enough to sleep.

He lay there, listening to Brock's heartbeat, holding everything he most wanted in the world.

They needed to end this bullshit. And soon.

———

"Are you really leaving, Brock?" James still sounded so tired, the man sitting heavy in his wheelchair. "Really?"

"For a bit, yeah." Brock shook his head. "We all need to recover." The wolf was with the cops. They could keep him out of trouble. "It's a vacation. That bastard's not giving anything up. Not a thing. Mick tried to get him to sing, but he swears it was all about the drug ring. Says he's the end of the line."

"What about the wife?"

"She's gone." Rey came in and leaned against James's chair.

"Gone? Where?" Griz sounded as grumpy as Brock felt.

"Just gone. Disappeared. Hank went to find her, and the house is empty. The car is still there. No activities on her phone or credit cards."

"Shit." That had a bad sound. People... disappearing. "The weasels?"

"The weasels, the cultists—they were all rounded up and are being processed. Most have been released."

"Shit again." Brock shook his head. "We need to get everyone to a safe place for a while. Separate ones, if need be. The office isn't it."

"I'm not moving again." James sounded so sure.

"Neither are we." And another nation was heard from, this time in the form of fox and wolf.

"Mick will watch over us." Rey smiled. "You'll be back?"

"Yeah. Of course. Griz and I just need alone time. Bond time." Time to hide and wallow and sleep. He felt like he never got any rest. Maybe he was still not completely recovered, like James. Griz seemed to think he needed sleep.

"What about Hank?" James asked. He'd been very... curious... about the bobcat kitty.

"He's back to work, as far as I've heard. He scrambled."

"Oh." James ducked his head. "Sure."

"He left his card here," Rey offered.

"Cool. Mick might need it. Any idea when my office will be back up?" James firmed his mouth, shoulders straightening.

"Soon. We're putting in a chair lift for you." Kit put one hand on James's shoulder.

"I won't be in this thing long," James stated, voice determined.

"No. We need to hunt together." He held James's gaze, knowing that they were both scared. James should be healed by now.

James nodded slowly. "Email?"

"I'll call and text. I just—we need to be together. Only us." He reached for Griz's hand.

"I'm jealous and proud, brother."

"It will happen for you."

James shook his head. "Not now, eh? Not now."

"Yes, but this is not forever." He bent to hug James tight. "I love you."

"I love you, brother. Take care of yourself."

"I have Griz for that." He grinned all around. "We need to go talk to Mick."

"He's pouting," Kit murmured. "Sulking."

"I'm not resigning. I'm taking a sabbatical. Six weeks and I'll be home."

"Promise." Rey held out a pinkie, and there was no way he could say no to the swear. He linked fingers.

"Promise."

"Good." Rey pushed into his arms and kissed his cheek. "Bring us back something cool."

"We will." Time to go check in with Mick. And go. The mountains were calling.

Griz nodded and wrapped one arm around him, dragging him out of room. "If you stay, we'll never go anywhere," Griz said gently. "Mick, and we're gone."

"Yeah."

They headed to Mick's temporary command center to knock on the door.

"Come!"

"I can't do this." He looked up into his mate's eyes. "Let's just go."

"Hey, we owe him this much." Griz grabbed his hand. "Come on. We can. Together."

He opened the door, bursting in with a growl. "I'm not quitting. I really want a vacation."

"I know." Mick turned to him, looking haggard for a minute, but then broke into a smile. "You deserve some rest, man. Healing. We got this here. Hetrick swears there's no one else coming for us."

"You're my pack." He launched into Mick's arms, rubbing cheeks. "We're pack. I want to bond with Griz."

"That's the most important thing, buddy. You're mates. Go get all together." Mick hugged him tight enough to make him grunt.

"I'll be close. If you need me...," he offered.

"He won't," Griz rumbled.

"No. No, we'll wait until James—well, we'll wait." Mick shrugged. "I feel like there's more to this. To both Patel and this guy, but damn. We need to lick our wounds, and I think we're safe enough for now. You know I'd never let you go if I didn't."

"All of us." He nodded, sighed. Mick had talked long and hard with Hetrick before the police had come. Maybe he knew something he wasn't telling. This was shockingly hard.

"I'll do some research while you guys are off." The hard note crept back into Mick's voice. "No one fucks with my team like this."

"No. No, watch yourself. Please." No one fucked with his team either.

"I will." Mick let him go. "Get out of here. Get a burn cell and don't let anyone know where you actually are."

"I swear. I'll be in touch. Later."

"Go." Mick pushed him away, patting his arms before turning from them.

"Griz?" He looked up at his mate, the sight of his lover swimming.

"Come on! Before he changes his mind." Griz whirled him up into those brawny arms and whisked him away.

Soon he was in their SUV, Griz blaring AC/DC on the radio, heading up into the mountains. He could breathe for the first time in days, and Brock just couldn't stop grinning even through his tears. "The mountains are calling us, huh?"

"They are, baby. I want to roll you in the snow."

Brock moved over, one hand sliding along Griz's leg. "I think I might have forgotten how to... roll."

"No!" Griz made an exaggerated horrified face. "I think I can relearn you."

"Better than returning me, right?"

"Not going to happen." One big hand covered his. "So not."

The heat buzzed around him, between them, and he moaned. Just this little bit of time alone, with no stress, was already working at them.

"The weather's getting colder, quick."

"I know!" Griz sounded so pleased. "Snuggles."

"Fucking before the fire?" he shot back.

"Yep. What kind of bed does this place have?"

"There's a loft that's all mattresses, believe it or not. I like to wallow."

"Oh. Will it hold me?" Griz had gone hopeful now. Wistful.

"Both of us, fuzzed-out. I swear." He'd had an entire family of bears in there a few years ago, hiding out.

"Oh, cool." When he glanced over, Griz's shoulders had relaxed visibly. "Man, I didn't even know I was tense."

"We'll be fine. This is the right thing to do, right?"

"It is. No guilt." Griz squeezed his hand. "Everything is on hold until everyone is ready to work again. You know that. We're all scattered."

"I just... this whole thing is fucking ridiculous. It makes me itch."

"I hear you." Griz's voice went all growly. "I'm sick of our team being a target."

He loved how fast Griz had become part of the group.

"But I need this, kit. I need our time. It pulls on me."

"Good." Brock was a selfish bastard, and he knew it. Griz was his.

"When do we stop?" Griz asked.

"We're almost there. Through Estes and then up."

Griz nodded, grinning over. "We can wait that long, right?"

Brock chuckled, because honestly, he'd been afraid he was just ready to give up on sex, but Griz's teases reminded him that he wasn't quite dead yet.

Not even as much as a little, really. Griz had a healing effect.

"I'm sorry I took so long, Griz. I was trying to...." He didn't know. Heal? Hide?

"I know." Griz shrugged. "And I ran. South America. Africa."

"Next time, take me?"

"Fuck yes." That emphatic agreement warmed him to his toes. "And not to work."

"No. No, take me to play with."

"Mmmm." The best sound ever was that deep rumble.

Brock began to come to life, his nerves waking up, his heart waking up. The shit he'd been poisoned with had been insidious, but worse had been the conviction that he'd tossed out the best thing in his life for a cheating, thieving fox.

"Stop it," Griz growled. "Don't make me bite you."

"I want you to." Hell, he would let Griz beat him for this if he had to.

"Do you? That can be arranged, kit. I want to eat you up."

"Mmm. Okay." He wasn't afraid to poke the bear. In fact, he loved it. "I want you to fuck me so good, I forget that anyone but you ever existed."

"Yes." Griz looked at the road, hands clenched so hard on the wheel, his knuckles had gone white.

"Thank you." He scooted closer, hand on Griz's leg.

"You're so very welcome."

God, he was going to explode before they got to Estes Park.

"No. No, you'll save it for me, kit. I've earned the pleasure."

"I will. I mean, you have." Brock laughed. "I love you."

"I love you. Here's Estes. Do we need to stop and provision?"

Brock sighed mournfully. "We do. I guess a quickie in the car is out of the question."

Griz looked out the window at the steel-gray clouds. "Not if we want to beat the snow."

"Damn." He would reward Griz for his diligent protection later.

"Yeah. I'll get the meats; you get the snacks." Griz pulled into the Safeway parking lot.

"On it." He hopped right out, wanting to get back on the road and settled before the storm broke.

Snacks—salty and sweet—and enough frozen berries to make his bear smoothies for six weeks. He could do that.

———

Griz loaded up a cart with meat. Steak and roast and chicken and hamburger. They would need it. Oh, fish.

Fish was always welcome with them, and he knew how to cook.

He got rainbow trout and salmon.

"Want that on ice?" the fish counter guy asked.

"Please." He had no idea how far they still had to travel.

He thought Brock was beginning to come back. The second kidnapping had cracked something deep down in his kit, and he didn't like it, but that familiar fire was coming around. They would get through this, go back to their team, and kick some ass.

But now, this time was theirs. This was a moment to hide and fuck and become a single heartbeat.

The idea made him smile so wide that people stared a little. Yeah, he was a bear. He could be a goofy big thing.

"Behind you, bear. You have a fine ass."

Griz wiggled it. Why not, if his kit was watching? He could show off.

A rush of desire flooded through their bond.

Oh. His cheeks heated, his heart kicking into high gear with its beat. Yeah. Hello.

"Almost done? I need you, bear."

"I am. Come on to the checkout." He grabbed Slim Jims and bread and jam and Hot Tamales on the way out.

Brock had done well himself—berries and cheese and crunchy things. They were a good team.

Oh, God, he was shopping for groceries with his mate. Like totally normal people.

He found himself standing taller, rumbling with pure joy.

Brock touched him on the small of the back when they got in line, brushing past him to help him unload the cart.

Tiny explosions trailed up along his skin, making him

shiver. Griz grunted at the aftershocks going up his spine and bursting in his head like tiny fireworks. Yum.

"Focus, bear. We have another twenty minutes' drive."

"I can do that." Griz pulled out his wallet to pay.

"Thank you." *"I'll make it up to you, mate."*

"You will. For days, at least." He nodded and smiled blandly at the cashier.

"Are you having a nice day, sir?" she asked.

"Lovely."

Brock grinned at him, the pure devil shining out of those bright green eyes. Griz frickin' lived for that smile.

"You two having a party?"

"Absolutely."

"Well, have fun." She winked at him, which made him flush again. Lord. At least she was nice. And she seemed to know when to keep her mouth shut.

"Thanks." Brock grabbed half the bags. "Come on, Griz."

"Yes, sir." He took the cart. He needed one hand free to goose his lover.

Which he did, hiding it with his body. God, this was fun!

Brock *rowl*ed at him, jumping and wiggling like a new lover. In a way they were, right? They needed to learn each other all over.

"Sweet kitty."

"I will bite you."

"Promise? I'll bite back."

Brock laughed for him, the sound of it pure joy. They got in the vehicle, and Griz dared take a kiss, which his kit gave without a second's hesitation.

"Take us home, bear."

"Tell me where to turn." He got them going, ready for that. Home. How long had it been since Griz had felt like he had one?

How the hell had he ended up with a mate with multiple houses?

"My grandfather."

"What?"

"My grandfather was a wealthy man, and I'm the only grandchild."

"No shit? My grandfather was a bear." He chuckled. "I mean, like a hermit who lived in a log cabin."

"Mine ran a huge telecommunications company and died worth millions."

"Wow." How did he not know that? "I like that you use it to buy places to stay."

"Property is a good thing. I like to have land."

"Territory." He nodded sagely. Not that he'd ever had any.

"Yes. We need it. I'll show you all of it, but you'll like this one best."

"I know I will." He glanced sideways. "You'll be there, baby."

"Of course I will, bear. Why would I...? Oh." He could see it when Brock understood him, and his mate beamed. "Oh, turn off here!"

Griz hit the turn, glad the road was still clear, even though a light snow had begun to fall.

The road—or the track, because it was barely even a wide bit in between the trees—led damn near straight up the mountain. He didn't figure they'd end up above the tree line, because Brock liked cover, but damn. The air was plenty thin.

"Breathe, bear. You're from this shit. I'm a jungle kitty."

"I am. I'm good. I'm just excited." Almost bouncing, which didn't go with driving.

"Uh-huh. Have some water, would you?"

"Sure." He broke open the seal of a bottle sitting in the console. "I'm fine."

"Good, because I intend to dump the cold stuff where it goes and then jump your ass."

"Yeah? We're not going for a five-mile run first?" he teased.

"You go for it. I'm going to stay in the warm."

"Oh, I wouldn't want to make you cold and lonely." That would never do.

"No? Good to know." Brock ran one hand along his thigh. "Slow down, the house is to the right."

"Got it." The A-frame rose out of a tiny hill, which would protect it from the wind.

It was a little like something from a storybook, like something from a Christmas movie. Those ones on the Hallmark Channel, dammit. This one would have a happy ending too.

"It's bigger than it seems. We'll have all we need."

"It looks perfect." He was being a sap, but Griz thought he was allowed. He pulled up in front of the garage, just taking everything in for a minute.

"Let me—" Brock tapped something out on his phone, and the garage door went up. "There."

"Wow. And a breezeway to the house and everything." This was the life. No block heater required, and no scraping the windshield.

"Yes. There's a cord of wood, and we have a deep freezer full."

"Bed. Blankets." Griz hopped out of the car once they parked, waiting to grab Brock as soon as he stepped out.

"Loft, bear. A whole soft loft for us." Brock reached for him.

"Now." Griz spun Brock around before kissing him soundly.

Brock pressed close, and Griz could feel his kit's hunger. "Groceries."

"I know." They would be civilized for another fifteen minutes....

Brock opened the back and started loading his arms with bags. For a little guy, he was strong. That wiry jaguar muscle was hot as hell.

He loved having the view of that pretty ass all the way up the stairs to the main floor. His turn now to wolf whistle and watch Brock wiggle. Hell yeah.

"Come up and help with the cold shit." The entire bottom floor was a huge open space with a vast fireplace. It was pure pine and leather and light.

"This is amazing." He turned in circles, taking it all in. The place had windows along the back, a huge leather sofa, a flat-screen TV, a recliner. There was a door leading to the back porch, one to what he assumed was a pantry, and another to what he hoped was a bathroom.

The cabin was... majestic. Huge.

"The loft is upstairs. You'll love it."

"I can see it from here." It was cozy, tucked away under the sloping eaves. Oh, he wanted up there.

"Go on, bear. I'll throw this stuff in the fridge."

"No. I can help." He needed to know where all the food was. Especially the honey.

The house was fairly well stocked, which made sense, as the house was warm, the wood was stacked high, and nothing smelled musty. Someone had called ahead to make things comfy for him. That was so damn sweet.

"Kiss me, baby."

"There's nothing I want more." Brock reached up, face titled to offer his lips.

The kiss went long and slow and hot enough to melt the frozen stuff. By unspoken agreement, they put the rest of the groceries away right after it ended.

Brock's hunger buzzed through their bond, his mate almost wild. Oh, they were going to have so much fun. No being too gentle either. They needed to tear each other up.

"Upstairs," his kit snarled. *"Now, bear."*

"Yes." He nodded, grabbing Brock and sprinting for the stairs.

He stopped when he got to the landing, staring. Brock hadn't been exaggerating—almost the entire floor was covered in mattress-grade cushions, blankets, and pillows. The ceiling had a huge skylight and then hundreds of sparkly, dangly ornaments hanging down.

Such a kitty. Or maybe part bird....

"Do you like it?"

"I love it so much." It was like Brock made into a not-human, real-world place. Just perfect. Griz began flinging off clothes.

Brock chuffed out a laugh, stripping down himself, baring that sweet, strong, scarred body.

All he could do for a moment was stare, hands hanging at his side. "Christ, you're amazing."

To his surprise, his lover blushed a deep, warm red, pleasure pouring between them. So sweet, his Brock. So brash and confident, but so uncertain underneath.

He held out one hand, reaching for his kit. "Need you."

"Yes." Brock's fingers twined with his.

He drew Brock to the huge bed, glad to note it was firm when he sank down. Of course, jaguars did love tree limbs, so maybe a soft bed was right out. Hell, with all the pillows and blankets, if they'd wanted soft, they could have soft.

They flopped down, laughing and rolling over and over. All that skin was his. He stretched Brock out, loving that there was room for them both here, a space for them.

Happiness sang in his heart, so Griz opened up their bond, letting it flow through as he touched his mate.

"Bear. Goddess, you make me dizzy."

"I want to make you kinda crazy. That's what you do to

me." He kissed Brock's chin, then pinched one hard little
nipple.

He lived to hear that low *rowl*, that sound that was part
need, part hunger, part warning. Yeah. That was worth explor-
ing. Gnawing.

Brock rolled them, landing on top of him with a thump.
"Bear. Do it again."

"Which part?" He got toothy, biting, then pulling at that
nipple again.

"Yes!" Brock straddled him, pushing back against his cock,
teasing the fuck out of him.

"Oh fuck, kit." He grabbed that tight ass, rubbing Brock
back and forth.

"Yes. Fuck me. I need it."

"God." They had lube? They had to have lube.

"Of course we have lube." Brock slid off him and crawled
to the edge of the bed, that pretty ass up in the air.

"Oh, good. I didn't buy any."

"I know. We didn't need to." Brock came back with a tube.

He missed seeing that backend offered up to him.

"Oh, you want to do me from behind?" Brock turned and
wiggled.

"Not this time, baby. I want you on top of me."

"This time." The satisfaction in the words made him
smile.

"Yeah. Next time I will tear up the floor with your knees, I
swear." He reeled Brock in. He was ready for the main event.
Now. His body wasn't going to wait much longer.

One hand found his cock, the touch blistering and almost
too good.

Griz shuddered. "Christ. Brock. More."

"Everything." Brock stroked him, base to tip, over and
over.

Griz found whatever skin he could almost blindly. Brock

was making him crazy with need. He tried to focus, to slick his fingers, but Brock's hand never slowed.

"I can't think when you do that, baby." Not one bit.

"Are we thinking?" Brock crawled over him, plucking the lube from his fingers.

"We are if we want to get you ready. I have to have brain-to-extremity communication." He watched with burning eyes as Brock slicked up his fingers.

"Extremity communication?" Brock's fingers disappeared behind him, and Griz grumbled with frustration, not being able to see.

"Gimme." He wanted to know what was going on back there.

"Hmm?" Oh, sexy kitty.

"Baby, I want to see you touch yourself." He growled the words, speech starting to slip away.

Brock turned halfway, showing off for him, letting him watch those fingers disappearing into Brock's hole. Then reappearing. It was hypnotic. Griz thought he might be drooling.

"Mine." The word buzzed through him. *"All mine."*

"Yes, bear. Yes." Brock panted, rocking on his own hand.

Now it was Griz's turn to touch, so he grabbed that bobbing cock, stroking hard.

"You're going to fuck me."

"I am. I swear. You need to lube me up too." That was a dare. A command.

"God, yes. Please." That felt so good, Brock's eager reach.

The feel of Brock coating him in cool gel was almost shocking against his skin. So damn good, and that would give him a tiny bit of control.

"Are you ready, bear? I need it. You. Your cock. Now."

"Yeah. Yeah. I need you." No more waiting. Not this time.

Brock climbed up to straddle him, eyes blazing as he knelt up tall.

"Beautiful man." He stroked Brock's chest and belly, loving the rough and smooth play of hair and skin, the raised scars.

"Love." Brock sank down, slow and easy, lips open as he sighed.

"Fuck, baby. Oh Jesus." That tight heat closed around him, and Griz had to grit his teeth to hold it.

"Yes. Take me. Please." Brock rolled his hips, rocking on his prick.

His balls drew up, but he kept going, needing to get some friction going. He'd be damned if he didn't make his mate come first.

Brock grunted out a laugh. "Greedy bear."

"Yes. Give me more."

"Anything." He yanked Brock down, really letting him feel everything. Brock yowled, the sound pure need. Yes. Yes, that was it. Now he just needed to touch that hot, hard cock again.

He grabbed it like a handle, stroking Brock, base to tip. Then he rubbed his thumb over the tip, gathering the wet drops there.

Mmm... he could feel how much his kit liked that, the pressure around his cock going wild.

So he did it again before pinching the slit closed.

"Bear!" Brock bucked atop him, rocking furiously.

"Love. Oh, love." He was incoherent, and at least half that was joy. His mate. His home. He could be here.

The other half was pure sex. So fucking good.

"Yes." Brock rode him like a fiend, like a wild pony. They slapped together so fast, he wouldn't be surprised to see smoke, and unbearable pressure was building in his balls.

Brock's eyes began to glow for him, the brightness making him gasp and groan. That cat was right there, and Brock scratched down his chest with blunt nails, making him arch up and grunt.

He rolled them, slamming down, driving into his mate, trusting that his lover was born to take him. They were bonded. He wouldn't hurt Brock. Not like this. He would just make Brock fly.

Brock's nails dug into his shoulders, his kit's head thrown back on a cry. "There!"

That was it. He hit that spot over and over, bending to bite at Brock's skin.

Brock screamed, the sound wild and fierce and utterly beautiful, the scent of spunk sharp on the air. He felt the force of it hitting his skin, and Griz roared, coming so hard, he saw stars, static bursting in his brain.

He slumped down, trusting Brock to take his weight, to hold him.

Brock cradled him with arms and legs, all but purring. "Mmmmate."

He grunted and snorted, nuzzling in and inhaling Brock's scent. The bear was right there on the edge of his body and mind, demanding its time.

Brock head-butted him gently, then rubbed their cheeks together, purring softly.

"Yes? Want to sleep with your cat."

Brock moaned softly, agreeing with him, moving away just long enough to shift. That long, slinky black cat was the most amazing thing, glowing green eyes blinking at him. Griz let the bear come, testing that loft with his grizzly weight.

It didn't even creak.

"Home, bear."

"Home." It filled all the empty places inside, just to hear it. He snuffled into the covers, tugging his cat in close. Naptime.

"Naps." That was the most satisfied sound he could imagine. The rest of the world, even the snow outside, could wait.

They were home.

EPILOGUE

Mick stood in his office, arms crossed, listening to the *tappity tap* of Carrie's nails against the keyboard in the outer room. He hated this. Hated it.

Okay, sure, he was back at work. The office had a state-of-the-art new security warning grid, extending twenty feet beyond the building, with booby traps and alarms on all ways in. Nothing, not even a were-cockroach, could get in.

James was back in his office, which Mick had spared no expense retrofitting for the wheelchair. James was healing, but his central nervous system was fucked right now.

He sighed. His team was splintered. Brock and Griz had disappeared to the mountains, and Dylan and Rey had requested a leave of absence. They were somewhere on the Gulf, sipping umbrella drinks.

He'd given his blessing to both, but it made him itch to be so far, to not be able to protect them.

What the fuck had happened? What had they really gotten into? He'd told them all he thought it was safe now Hetrick was in custody, but he knew better. Just like the tiger Patel,

Hetrick was afraid of something bigger than him, and Mick knew it. He smelled it. He'd lied to his fucking team.

A sound close by startled him, and he whipped around, snapping out a warning, and huge brown eyes stared at him.

"What do you want, Kit?"

"I made Guinness stew for you with extra carrots."

He relaxed his clenched hands. "Yeah? Thanks, kiddo. I love that." Stout stew was like an ancestral memory for him. Soothing.

"I know." Kit offered him a careful smile. "There's bread too. Do you want to come eat with me, or do you want to eat in here?"

He wavered, but Kit held out a hand, pleading in his gaze, and Mick nodded. "I'll come with you, huh? I miss a meal with my team."

Kit nodded back, but slowly. "Carrie and James...."

"They're eating at their desks."

"Yeah." Kit sighed. "I'll bring your bowl in. It's cold in the kitchen anyway."

"Hey, come on. We'll go get it and take it up to my couch." Poor Kit looked so down, those wide shoulders slumped and rounded. That wasn't gonna do.

"Yeah?" It took so little to perk the kid up.

"Yep. Butter. Bread. Stew." Hell, he'd cuddle. Kit was an incredible napper. Not like he was getting any work done.

"Butter, bread, stew. I got a new movie to watch even...."

Kit was remarkably uncritical of his media. It was hilarious. "Okay, move it, mister." He tugged Kit out of his office, that big hand still cradling his.

The world was crumbling at the edges, but the core was solid. He had to believe that.

He squeezed Kit's hand, the scent of stew like a drug.

He really did have to believe. There was no other option.

WANT MORE?

Julia Talbot

Join the Spurs and Shifters Newsletter for free stories, news, and contests from Julia Talbot and BA Tortuga!
https://lp.constantcontact.com/su/A9CRUzp/baand julia

Afterword

Hey, folks!

Thanks so much for reading my book! I'm so glad you made it here. If you liked the book, I hope you'll consider leaving a rating or review at your retailer of choice or adding the book to your Goodreads shelf.

If you're interested in more of my books, or in news about when they come out and what's coming soon, please check out my Facebook Group https://www.facebook.com/groups/juliatalbot/ or my newsletter here: https://lp.constantcontact.com/su/A9CRUzp/baandjulia

XXOO and Keep reading!

Julia Talbot

Also by Julia Talbot

Alpha Tales

An Alpha in Sheep's Clothing

Packmate for Hire

Too Many Alphas

Apex Investigations

Fox and Wolf

Jaguar and Grizzly

Mountain Lion and Bobcat

Alpha and Bear

Apex Security

Solids and Stripes

Dead and Breakfast

Fangs and Catnip

Fangs for the Memories

Home for the Howlidays

Full Moon Dating

New Moon

Isaiah and Jameson

Grizzly List

Bear Wanted

One and Only Bear

Bearly Working

Midnight Rodeo

Big Bear, Little Bear

Light a Rocket

Vampire Protection

The Dragon's Dilemma

Up in Flames

Nose to Tail, Inc.

Wolfmanny

Wolf's Man Friday

Wolf Maneuvers

The Peculiars

The Curse of the Mummy's Heart

The Shadow of the Count

Riding Cowboy Flats

Jackass Flats

Just a Cowboy

Riding the Circuit

Summit Springs

High Side

* * *

Contemporary

Catching Heir

Chef on Chef

Drive Your Truck

Home for the Hollandaise

Jumping, Landing, and Taking

Loose Snow

Love Dot Com

One More Yule Log

Out of the Frying Pan

Perfect

Sparkle and Shine

Historical

A Gentleman of Substance

A Pirate's Paradise

Offerings

Partners on the Trail

Post Obsession

Remembering Pleasure

To Hell You Ride

The White City

Paranormal

Bad Dog

Blue Moon Bar

Faster Bobcat

Link to the Crescent

Night of the Living Manny

Pack Mates

The Fire Inside

About the Author

Julia Talbot lives in the great Southwest with her wife and four basset hounds. A full-time author, Julia writes paranormals and more with lots of love and action and, as her alter ego Minerva Howe, she writes mpreg and alpha/omega stories. She believes that everyone deserves a happy ending, so she writes about love without limits, where all of her stories leave a mark.

Visit Julia's website: http://www.juliatalbot.com

9 798223 815853